HOW TO HAVE AN AFFAIR

BOOKS BY MICHAEL HEMMINGSON

FOR BORGO PRESS / WILDSIDE PRESS:

The Rose of Heaven
In the Background Is a Walled City
Barry N. Malzberg: Beyond Science Fiction
Judas Payne

FOR OTHER PRESSES:

The Naughty Yard (Permeable Press, 1994)
Crack Hotel (Permeable Press, 1995)
Minstrels (Permeable Press, 1997)
The Mammoth Book of Short Erotic Novels (Carroll & Graf, 2000)
The Mammoth Book of Legal Thrillers (Carroll & Graf, 2001)
Wild Turkey (Forge, 2001)
The Comfort of Women (Blue Moon, 2002)
The Dress (Blue Moon, 2002)
Seven Women and Other Stories (Bookspan, 2003)
My Fling with Betty Page (Eraserhead Press, 2003)
Drama (Blue Moon, 2003)
The Rooms (Blue Moon, 2003)
The Lawyer (Blue Moon, 2003)
House of Dreams Trilogy (Avalon, 2004)
The Garden of Love (Blue Moon, 2004)
Expelled from Eden: A William T. Vollmann Reader (Thunder's
    Mouth Press, 2004)
The Las Vegas Quartet (Avalon, 2006)
Short & Sweet (Blue Moon, 2006)
Understanding William T. Vollmann (Univ. of South Carolina Press,
    2008)
Star Trek: TV Milestone (Wayne State Univ. Press, 2008)
The Yacht People (Neon Books, 2008)

HOW TO HAVE AN AFFAIR

AND OTHER INSTRUCTIONS

by

MICHAEL HEMMINGSON

The Borgo Press
An Imprint of Wildside Press

MMVII

FIRST EDITION

CONTENTS

For Princess Jolene of Hollywood...

fellow smut writer,
expert on the art of having affairs

SEXUAL PERVERSITY ON A TRAIN GOING TO CHICAGO

INTRODUCTION

Inside, Sharon Thomas knew there was a dirty, skanky slut waiting, wanting, to come out and go wild; the problem: she'd only slept with two men, at the tender age of nineteen, and she was too shy to approach anyone for sex. Her whore persona remained in her mind, creating nasty adventures as she lay in bed, fucking herself with a silver vibrator.

INSIDE THE PASSENGER CAR

For the first time in her life, Sharon was on a train. She was en route to a university in Chicago for an interview; she had the grades, the recommendations, and they wanted a face-to-face. Taking the train seemed like an adventure. She wore a short skirt and a sweater. She was a quite attractive and alluring, there's no doubt about it—much of it was an air of innocence about her, and the fact that this young woman had no desire to be innocent, she really wanted to be bad.

A man named Gerald Rhines knew this.

Gerald was forty-eight and on his second marriage; he was returning to the windy city from a business trip. His second marriage was in danger because he had a nasty knack for fucking other women. He couldn't help it; he loved women. He loved his wife, as much as he loved the first one. It wasn't like these "other" women meant anything to him; he met them when he traveled (which was required often in his job: regional sales rep for an academic publishing company) and many of them were married as well, these women, out to have a little meaningless fun. They tended to be younger than him.

Gerald liked younger women—what man didn't? He noticed Sharon in the bar section of the diner car, ordering a mixed drink. He was discreet, following her back to her seat. She seemed to be alone. He liked the way she glanced out the window, at the passing land—her naiveté.

He got himself a drink, returned, and sat across from her.

"No one's sitting here?"

"No."

"Do you mind?"

"No."

Sharon was attracted to him from that moment; she didn't let it show, of course. Older men made her circumspect; they'd made the moves on her before, but she'd never succumbed. She was going to play it cool with this one. She knew what was on his mind, the way he was looking at her. She crossed her legs for the effect—and yes, his eyes quickly glanced down, the skirt riding high. Maybe he saw her underwear? She hoped so.

"What are you drinking?" he asked.

"White Russian." She stared out the window, sipped her White Russian. She asked, "What're you drinking?"

"Tom Collins."

"Oh."

"Ever have one?"

"No."

"You should."

"It has a lime and a cherry in it."

He said, "I'm Gerald."

She liked the streaks of gray in his dark hair. She said, "Sharon."

They talked a little—why were they on this train? She told him about the interview.

"I had fun in college," he said.

"I bet you did."

"Can I get you another drink?" he offered.

She noticed her glass was empty. "Well."

"A White Russian?"

"I'll try a Tom Collins."

He took her glass. She sat there, wondering what the hell she was doing. The man was twice her age! More even! Maybe he wouldn't come back. Her nipples were hard under the sweater.

Gerald returned with a Tom Collins for her, a White Russian for himself. This made her laugh. She really did like him, and because she liked him, she allowed what happened next to happen.

She said she had to go to the bathroom. She gave him her empty glass, made her way to the bathrooms. She didn't know Gerald was following her. At the women's restroom, he pushed her in, closed the door and kissed her. They kissed for a good long minute, his hands on her back and her ass. Their lips parted; they looked at each other.

"I'm sorry," he said, "I couldn't help myself."

She thought: *Am I really doing this?*

The bathroom was very small. Gerald was quick to get to business. He lifted her, sat her butt on the sink. He pushed her skirt up, yanked her panties off. His cock was red and hard; it was thick with veins and had a giant head. Sharon was worried; the two young men she'd previously has sex with didn't have cocks the width of Gerald's. She wondered if it would hurt, if she could stretch that much. She heaved when he put it in her, almost telling him to take it out. He told her to relax and she did, her cunt forming comfortably around the thing. But it wasn't easy. Fortunately, the whole matter was quick—a three-minute fuck, really, but she came twice, and he came inside her. He kissed her on the nose when he was done. He bunched her panties, put them in the pocket of his suit jacket. "That was great," he said. He left the bathroom, left her alone there. Just like that.

She sat on the toilet and let Gerald's semen drip out of her.

She walked back to her seat and realized she had no underwear and Gerald's discharge was still coming out. It started to run down her thigh. She hoped no one noticed, and wasn't sure if she cared. She found her seat. He wasn't there. She thought he would be. She reached into one of her bags, found tissue, and cleaned the cum from her leg, being discreet.

Gerald appeared then, and sat down next to her.

MOTION

"Listen," he said, "close your eyes and just listen."

"Okay."

"Are your eyes closed?"

"Yes," she said.

"Listen to the train. Listen to the machinery."

"It's sexy," she said. Her hand reached over to his crotch.

THREE WEEKS LATER

"Are you following me?"

Sharon jumped, and turned. It was Gerald, on the train. She couldn't believe this. She couldn't help it—she embraced him, and kissed him.

"Hey, hey," he said.

"I'm sorry," she said. She blushed. She looked around. No one was watching.

Gerald straightened his tie.

"What are you doing here?" Sharon asked.

"I was wondering the same."

"Another interview at another college," she told him.

"Work," he said. "The usual."

He was looking her over. She was wearing a long skirt this time, and a sheer-fabric blouse, black bra showing through. He leaned forward and whispered, "Wish to go into the bathroom, my dear?"

She could only nod.

He led the way to the men's restroom. He opened the door, and—to her surprise—roughly shoved her in. Her face hit the wall. She breathed in. She turned to him. His face was carnal. He grabbed her by the hair, pulled her to him, and kissed her. "You little bitch," he said, "you horny little bitch."

"Yes," she said.

"Say this: 'I'm a horny little skank.'"

"I'm a horny little skank."

"A slut."

"A slut."

"I'm."

"I'm."

"A."

"A."

"Little."

"Little."

"Fuck bunny."

She laughed.

He pulled her hair harder. "What's so funny?"

"Kiss me," Sharon begged.

"I'll do more than that," he said, and kissed her. His hands were under her skirt, pulling her panties down.

"Gerald, wait," she told him. "I'm on my period."

"I might like that."

"I don't."

"I'll fuck your behind."

"What?"

He squeezed her rear end. "I'll fuck your little brown bunny," he said. He pushed her toward the sink, and played with her ass. He bent, and kissed the flesh. There wasn't enough room in here for this. He tried to stick a finger into her. Sharon flinched.

"You're a virgin here," he said.

She didn't know what to say.

"No one has broken your ass cherry yet?"

"No," she said, ashamed.

"Sit on the toilet," he ordered her, and she did. He had his cock out, just as huge and veined as she remembered. "Suck it," and he grabbed her hair; "suck it right now."

She took him in her mouth, eyes opened; she wanted to see all of this, even though his eyes were closed. Both his hands were on her head, pushing her so that she had to keep taking his cock in deeper with each penetration of her mouth. She gagged. Salvia drooled out of her mouth and on his penis. He opened his eyes once. Looking into those eyes, she knew, right then, that she could love this man— that she *would* love this man. It was one of those things. He closed his eyes again and continued to roughly fuck her mouth. Her lips were burning. Gerald started to come. As she ate his discharge, something very strange happened— she began to pee. She had no control. Piss flowed out of her, into the toilet, and it made her scream—a muffled scream. She pulled back, his cock popped out of her mouth and she spat cum onto his crotch as she had an orgasm and urinated simultaneously. She pressed her face into his pubes, catching her breath. Gerald stroked her hair.

"Lick up the mess," he said, softly.

She looked at the sticky cum on his pubic hair, his stomach. She stuck out her tongue and lapped away.

After a while, Gerald pulled up his underwear and slacks.

Sharon stood, noting that her tampon had slipped out, fallen into the toilet. She took another from her purse. She was self-conscious, but Gerald wanted to watch. She put the new one in, crouching, skirt hiked up. She was about to put her panties on and he stopped her.

"Let me keep them," he said; "a memento."

"You did that last time."

"I do it all the time."

"You must have quite a collection."

"You think I do this a lot?"

"I'll be naked under my skirt," she said.

"*That's* the idea."

"Okay," she said. "Okay."

"Here," he said. He took some toilet paper, wadded it, and wiped traces of semen off her chin. "We don't want people to see this. That wouldn't be decent."

"Yeah," she said, "they'll just see my cunt."

"It's a wonderful view," he noted.

GOLDEN HEART AND SOUL

She had lunch with him in the dining car. She was hungry. She had a bacon sandwich and Gerald had a baked potato, smothered in cheese and sour cream. The train rocked beneath them; like sex, she thought. What she really wanted was to be back in that bathroom. Gerald could tell.

"The wonderful part," he said, "is when you began to piss."

She looked at her sandwich.

"This bothers you?"

"It was so strange," Sharon said, voice low. "I didn't think I had to go. Maybe because I was sitting on the toilet."

"Maybe."

"It was weird."

"But you liked it."

"Yes."

"Look at me."

She did.

"It was very sexy," he said.

"It felt sexy."

"I wish I could've had my mouth on your cunt," he told her. "To taste it."

"Really? That's weird."

"You're so young."

She made a face. "Don't say that."

"But you are."

"I don't say: 'You're so old.'"

"I *am* old, honey," he said.

"Does it matter?"

"You have a good attitude," Gerald said. "You are a good person. You have a golden heart and soul."

"I want you to fuck me," she whispered. "I want to suck your fat dick again."

"Have you ever been fucked while on your period?"

"Yes," she said. "I don't like it."

"Why?"

"Blood."

"It's only blood."

"Blood on a cock?"

"I like blood on my cock. And other nasty things."

"You're testing me," she said.

"No."

"I'll do anything with you. You know more than me. So teach me." These words felt so alien coming out of her mouth.

THE SECOND MAN

"He's looking at you," Gerald said.

"Who?"

"That man."

"I know," Sharon said. "He's been looking at me for a while."

They were at the bar. Sitting at the counter. The man, in a dark suit, sat across from them. Sharon was drinking wine; Gerald had a martini.

"He's handsome."

"He's okay."

"He's handsome," Gerald said again.

"Yeah? So why don't *you* fuck him?"

"*You're* going to fuck him."

Sharon sipped her wine.

"I know you want to." He leaned close to her ear. "Close your eyes, and listen to the train."

She did.

"You're hot," he said.

"I'm *wet*," she said.

"You will fuck him."

"You *want* me to fuck another man?"

"I want you to *fuck*," he said.

She opened her eyes. "So what do we do? Go over there, make a proposition?"

"Don't be coy."

"This is your game, Master."

"We don't want him to feel set-up. We want it to seem natural. We'll go back to our seats and wait a bit. Ten minutes. You'll come back, alone, and let it play as it lays."

They left the bar. Sharon quickly glanced at the man; he was admiring the contour of her ass. She made eye contact.

THE INDECENT ENCOUNTER

His name was Andrew and he didn't take too long to approach her. Sharon was at the counter, having another glass of wine, alone this time. Andrew used the excuse to get another drink and sit next to her. Sharon ignored him.

"I can't drink wine," he said.

She sighed. "Why?"

"Bad memories."

"Wine?" She looked at him.

"Silly high school nights."

"So what do you drink now?"

"Bloody Marys."

"I prefer margaritas."

"Can I get you one?"

"I'm drinking wine."

He nodded. "Can I ask you something?"

"Sure."

"Your name."

"Sharon."

He told her his name.

They drank.

"Can I ask you something again?"

"Sure."

"The guy you were here with, not long ago," he said.

"Yeah?"

"Husband?"

"No."

"Boyfriend?"

"No.

"Lover?"

"Eh."

"Father? Uncle?"

"Why do you ask?"

"Stranger?"

"You're the stranger," she said.

"Okay, so this is bad," he said.

"Why is it bad?"

"I'm making a fool of myself."

"What's a fool?"

He laughed.

"Funny?"

"You're beautiful," he said.

"So are you," she said.

"I'm going to see my mother."

"That's nice."

"She's dying."

"I'm sorry."

"Cancer," he said. "Stomach."

"Oh," she said.

"You don't want to hear this."

"No," she said, "I don't."

"I'd like to kiss you," he said.

"Not in public."

"Where else would we kiss on a train?"

"We could always squeeze into a bathroom."

"Really?"

"You're not as naive as you act," she said.

"I never picked up anyone on a train," he confessed.

"No? It's fun. Right?"

"What?"

She leaned forward. "Isn't this fun?"

"It is," he said.

She whispered, "Wish to go into the bathroom, my dear?"

He said, "Yes."

She took his hand, and led him into the women's restroom. Once in, she pushed him against the wall, his face hitting it. She locked the door. He turned around. She slapped him across the face "Kiss me," she said, "you dirty pervert."

17

She grabbed his head, and brought their mouths together.

"It's so cramped in here," Andrew said.

"Yeah." Sharon got down on her knees. She undid his trousers, pulling them down, as well as his boxers. His thin, curved cock sprang in front of her face. It stank of sweat. She took it in her mouth. She was afraid he was going to come fast. She got up, pulled her skirt up and leaned against the sink.

"No underwear," he said.

"You noticed."

He saw the tampon string dangling out of her. "Um."

"Hurry," she said, "fuck me."

He grabbed her hips, and shoved his cock into her. It was all very fast. There was blood.

They exited the restroom and didn't say a word to each other, didn't look at each other, went their separate ways.

She found Gerald and sat down next to him.

He ignored her the rest of the way to Chicago.

She felt like a dirty, skanky slut and she liked it.

THE END OF CELIBACY

Hannah had a quirky look to her I found appealing—thick, dark-rimmed glasses; a white streak in her otherwise jet black hair; an odd-assortment of attire, cool in this age of the awkward. She was one of the regulars who hung out at the pub down the street from my apartment. Some friends were playing pool, which wasn't my thing. Hannah bought a pitcher of beer and we sat together.

A guy was bending, ready to take a shot at the table, his rear end very close to us. "Get your butt somewhere else," Hannah said, "or I'll take a pool stick and shove it up"

"That's not very nice," I said. "How'd you like it if someone stuck a pool stick in your ass?"

Hannah raised her brows. "I just might like it."

That was the first clue I didn't get—I wasn't paying attention. I'd recall in hindsight, yes, as well as overhearing her talk about how her favorite scene in *Last Tango in Paris* was when Marlon Brando put butter up his young lover's backdoor before sodomizing her.

Soon the beer was gone.

"What will you do now?" Hannah said.

"Don't know," I said.

She took her glasses off and looked at them. "I live a block away, you know."

"No," I said, "I didn't know. So do I."

This was the second clue—and I wasn't paying attention.

"Well," she said.

"Maybe we can go there," I said.

She put her glasses back on. "Okay."

We walked up the block to her place, a small cottage. It was nice, a little messy. I asked how much she paid for it.

"Nothing," she said. "My parents own the property."

"Nice."

"I have beer, I think," she said, going to the kitchen.

I sat on the couch in the small living room.

Hannah returned with two Budweisers. "Yes, I have beer."

She sat next to me.

I don't remember what we talked about. On the floor, I noticed an action figure of the Warner Brothers Martian from the Bugs Bunny cartoon. "I always loved that Martian," I said.

"Me too," she said, going to the floor and picking it up. "Marvin the Martian. *'I'm going to destroy planet Earth!'*" I touched her hair. She put her head in my lap. It was nice to touch somebody.

"I, um, I don't know what to do," I said.

"What?"

"I haven't been with anyone in a while."

"I don't believe that."

"It's true."

"It's a line," she said. "Do you like me?"

"Yes," I said.

"I like you." She got on the couch with me and we began to kiss. She had to take her glasses off, they were getting in the way. We kissed for a long time. She pushed me back on the couch, and lay on top of me. I grabbed her ass, put my hands down her skirt.

She pulled her mouth from mine. "*Bad* boy," she said.

I grabbed her head, and we kissed more.

When I tried to touch her cunt, she stopped me.

"No," she said.

"Sorry," I said.

"Don't worry about it," she said, and we kissed.

When I touched her breasts over the fabric of her blouse, she pushed them away. "Now, now," she said.

"Sorry," I said.

She took one of my hands and put it back on her ass. "Play with that."

I did, and we kissed. My hand, and my second hand, were all over her butt.

"Hey," Hannah said, "rub my asshole."

"What?"

"With your finger," she said, and I found her asshole with my finger. "In small circles," she said, "yeah, like that"

She pulled away from me, and sat. She took the finger I'd been rubbing her with, put it in her mouth, sucked on it. She smiled, and gave my finger back. She put her glasses on.

"What's wrong?" I asked, moving to her, wanting to kiss her more.

"Nothing," she said. "I have to pee."

"Hey." I grabbed her hand as she stood up. "Can I watch?"

"You want to watch me pee?"

"Yes," I said.

"I need a commitment before I go that far," she said.

"We hardly know each other."

"Exactly," she said, and went to the bathroom.

I sat there.

I got up, and followed. The door was unlocked, and I went in. Hannah was sitting on the toilet; she glanced up at me. She smiled and said, "You." I could hear the stream of her urine. I sat on the floor, cross-legged.

"You're bold," she said.

"The door was unlocked."

"There *is* no lock."

"I couldn't resist."

She stood up. "Okay, Mr. Bold. Clean me."

"With my mouth?"

"*Ab*solutely not."

I would've done it with my moth, if she'd asked. I took a wad of toilet paper, and wiped her cunt. She pulled her panties up.

"I have to go too," I said.

"Then I get to watch," she said. *"Quid pro quo."*

She took my place on the floor; I stood in front of the toilet, took my cock out.

Hannah made a weird sound. She moved, snagged my cock, and put her mouth before it, drinking my urine; what she didn't get flowed out, down her chin, and into the bowl. I liked the sound this made. I breathed hard; it was an experience in itself watching her drink from me.

She pressed her face to my leg. "I'm sorry. I couldn't help myself," she said, softly. "Now you know my fetish. Okay, I'm weird. You'll never love me."

"I could love you," I said.

"Do you mean that?"

"Yes."

"Will you kiss me to prove it?" she asked.

"Yes," I said.

She stood, and we kissed, and I tasted her—and me.

"I want to make love to you," I said.

"No, I can't," she said.

Hannah left the bathroom and sat on the edge of her bed. I sat next to her; we both fell back. It was a nice, big, comfortable bed, the kind of bed I liked; the kind of bed I didn't have.

"It's late," she said, moving away from me. "I'm a little drunk."

"Me too," I said.

"You can stay here," she said, "if you want."

"I'd like that."

"I'd like it too," she said, standing. "I'm going to turn the light off."

"Okay."

In the dark, I saw her silhouette; she was removing her clothes. I also took my clothes off, and got under the covers. She joined me; we didn't touch. My hand went to her body; she was still wearing her bra and panties. I moved closer to her, kissed her.

"I don't think I want to screw," she said.

"Okay," I said.

"I mean, I'm not sure if I can."

"Okay."

"I'm not sure if I'm in the right frame of mind."

"Okay."

"It's not *okay*," she said, "you don't understand, you don't know."

"I *want* to," I said.

"I know you do."

"Hannah," I said.

"It's nice having you in my bed," she said.

"It's nice to be in a bed with someone." She placed her head on my chest, and then a hand, playing with the hair. We were quiet, touching each other. Her hand moved down, and grasped my cock.

"This is nice," she said.

"Yes," I said, "it is."

"Nice...."

I kissed her on the head.

"I know," she said, and, "I'm twenty-eight years old."

"Yeah?"

"I'm still a virgin."

I laughed, after a moment.

"This is true," she said.

"Now *who* is giving *who* a line?"

She let go of my cock. "I made up my mind years ago that I would save myself for my husband, because some day I plan to marry a nice man. And this man will expect me to be a virgin."

"I see."

"No you don't see," she said. "I don't expect you to understand. Other men haven't. Like I said, I'm twenty-eight. This doesn't mean I'm not sexual. *Obviously I'm sexual, and I have fetishes.* I'm really pretty basic in that matter—I have a pee fetish, and a butt, you know. I mean, I'm a virgin, *vaginally,* but I like having sex in my butt."

I didn't know what to say.

"I'm terribly attracted to you," she went on. "I want you. I want you inside me. But I want more than a fuck-buddy. I had a fuck-buddy for a while, for a few months, it was just sex, nothing more. I didn't like it; I mean it was okay, but it wasn't me. It was a different me."

"He fucked you in the ass?"

"Yes. I don't know if he liked it that much. Some men do, some don't."

I'd only had anal sex with a woman once, and I think I was nineteen or twenty.

"I want you to fuck me," Hannah said, "but I'm looking for more than just fucking. I'm not looking for a husband. I'll do that in my thirties, maybe my forties. I'm looking for companionship, closeness, a little love. Devotion, all that."

"Sounds nice," I said.

"Yes. It sounds—it sounds nice." She took her panties off. "I'd like you to fuck me," she said. "I want you to."

"Lubricant?" I asked, thinking the last time I'd done this, I had to use a lot of petroleum jelly.

"Spit is fine," Hannah said. She spit into her hand, put her hand between her ass cheeks. She spit into her hand again, and rubbed the saliva over my cock. "I'm getting impatient," she said.

I moved on top of her, feeling inexpert. Hannah reached back, took my cock, and guided me into her ass—where it slid in just fine, without hesitation or resistance. The warmth of her interior sent a tingle up my body and soul. Hannah whispered, "Oh boy," and pushed her rear up, hard, slamming into my pelvis. I looked down at the streak in her hair, which was scattered about the back of her neck and on the bed with the rest of her hair. I swear she had an orgasm, I wasn't sure, but mine came quickly, and it was a lot; I emptied myself inside her.

We lay next to each other after, and Hannah commented on the amount of semen I'd gushed out, that she liked how it felt up her ass, and coming out her ass.

She touched and played with my cock and balls, and soon I was hard again. She got on top of me. "This position is always tricky," she said, sitting down on my cock and sliding it in. She leaned forward to kiss me, and it popped out, covered in semen from that first ejaculation. Hannah giggled, and put my cock back in her. I reached for the light. "What are you doing?" she said.

"I want to see you."

"I like the light off."

"Okay."

"Oh, turn it on if you want."

I did. She still wore her bra; her hair was a mess. I reached to unclasp her bra and she pushed my hand away; my cock slipped out of her.

"Let's try it like this," I said, gently pushing her off me and onto her back. I put her legs on my shoulders; I didn't need her help to find my way in. I was deep in her now.

"I like this," she said.

"I can kiss you," I said, and did.

"Kiss me more."

I did.

"Fuck me harder."

I did, and I came inside her again.

"I have to piss," I said to her, "do you want it?"

She made a noise, reached up and bit my right nipple, hard.

"Ouch," I said.

We went back to bed, in each other's arms, and fell asleep.

I woke up, the next morning, with Hannah messing around with my ass. She had her face down there—I was lying sideway—slicking from my balls to my crack. I'm not sure how long she'd been doing this, but it was a nice thing to wake up to. She pushed me onto to my stomach, spreading my buttocks, a light finger on my sphincter, then a tongue. She licked it a bit, asked me if I liked that. I did, of course—"Yes," I said. She said, "I like it too," and licked more, harder this time, pushing the tip of her tongue into me like a thirsty animal at a waterhole. I felt saliva roll down onto my balls—a funny, ticklish feeling. She started to suck, making sounds that I can only describe as pleasantly perverse. She did this for the good part of an hour, as I lay there in ecstasy, having discovered a new world. She was still making wicked sucking sounds, and there was a soft hum from the back of her throat. She turned me over, and sucked on my cock for a bit. "My mouth is getting tired," she said, "can you fuck me?" She was on her hands and knees, and I took her from behind. I grabbed her hips, and slammed myself inside and out of her. I wanted to come in her mouth, this image was in my head. I told her this. She turned around and took me in her mouth, and I came.

And that's how I ended my period of celibacy.

THE INSTALLATION

I.

Kathleen Barter, an American student working on her Ph.D. in cultural anthropology and postcolonial theory, woke up inside her London flat one day and realized she was broke, she was in trouble; the only thing she had that could possibly save her was the pink little wet thing with lips that resided between her legs; she was twenty-eight-years old, pale and petite with very small breasts and skinny legs and raven-black, greasy hair and she still wore braces because of her crooked teeth so people thought she was fifteen or so, and her passport was always scrutinized as being a fake when she went to a pub for a pint of Guinness, the only liquor she drank. Some of the men she met at the bars would give her money, but it was always £10-20 and that was nothing, really; quid to last for a day…she needed more…much more…*she was not a prostitute*…but her rent was two months past due, her credit cards were over the limit, the electricity company was going to shut off the lights, the U.S. government wasn't going to give her anymore financial aid because she had not made progress on her thesis…she had no job and little in her checking account…so she had an idea. She placed an ad in the paper; the ad read:

FEMALE WILL DO ANYTHING FOR £5,000

II.

"What I want you to do, dear, is masturbate in public," Edward Kaff told Kathleen during their first meeting at his lavish house in the Whitechapel area, "in front of all my friends, colleagues, ex-lovers, business partners, enemies, critics and curious on-lookers. It will be part of an art exhibit, of course—a very snooty, very snitty, very uptight sort of exhibit that I want to put a bit of arse-kicking into. You, in fact, will be part of the exhibit, *you will be a work of art*, an installation lying there naked on the floor in front of everyone and diddling your clit for, oh, an hour, maybe an hour and a half."

"Okay," said Kathleen.

"Have I lost you let?"

"Not yet."

"I need a pretty girl, like you. Not a model, not someone so…perfect." Just a regular young lady like yourself. You are the sort of young lady I am, in fact, looking for. You're very pretty, as they say in the vernacular."

"Thank you."

"But…now I have to tell you the finale; this is a big art show and my sixtieth birthday party—the finale is I will get naked with you and, by the bye, fook the *fuque* out of you."

"Okay."

"In front of everyone."

"Okay."

"And I don't mean some wham-bam-thank-you-ma'am sort of deal. It will be a long, sweaty, *healthy* fuck. I may be an old man but I'm in top shape and practice Tantric love-making techniques. Do you know what this is?"

"Is it like Feng Shui?"

"I can go on up to six to eight hours of straight pussy, ass, and mouth-pounding and not ejaculate."

"Oh."

"How does that sound?"

"Sounds interesting."

"You don't have a problem with an old man like me?"

"No," Kathleen said.

"After all, your ad said 'anything'."

"And I meant it."

"So what do you say, first impression?" he asked.

"I think it's something to think about," she said.

"Go home and "think" on it, pretty little thing," he said, "but I need an answer in the next day or so…the exhibit is in two weeks…if you don't want to, I need to find another young lady. If I have to, I'll hire a call girl. But I'd rather have…someone like you."

III.

She called Edward Kaff and told him yes, she would take the job.

"Good," said Kaff; "good."

"I guess we should talk arrangements…."

"I have a simple contract ready for you to sign, half a page long, straight to the point. I'll pay you half upon signing—that's £2,500—and the other half will be paid upon completion of the art project."

"Okay," said Kathleen, "okay."

"The rest, we need to discuss in person."

"When?"

"When is good for you, dear?"

"Anytime. When is good for you, Mr. Kaff?"

"None of that mister stuff, girl, you can just call me Edward." Can you come to my house in, oh, three hours?" he asked.

She said: "Yes."

"We'll seal the deal then."

IV.

Indeed, the contract was simple: at the art show, she would whack-off for no less than an hour and no longer than two hours, using her hands and various dildos that would be provided; she would do this in front of the people there and she would not stop; then she would engage in up to, but not exceeding, five-to-eight hours of sexual intercourse with Edward Kaff: *basically a live sex show.*

She signed the form and Kaff handed her a check for £2,500.

She looked at the check and thought: *This will save my life.*

She could cash it and take off, go on the road, to Greece maybe, start her life anew somewhere, forget the past.

But a deal was a deal.

And she could use the other half.

What the hell, all she had to do was fuck this guy.

"How do you feel about intergen sex?" Kaff asked her.

She shrugged.

"Oh tell me."

"I don't know if I have any feelings."

"Have you ever slept with a man my age?"

"I don't think so."

"You don't *know*?"

"No," she said, getting annoyed, "I never have."

"We cannot go into this particular piece of art blind," he told her; "like any performance, we need to rehearse for the show. This is why I wanted to get started now. Do you understand?"

"I think, yes."

"Good. Get undressed."

She looked at him like he was a naughty uncle peeking in on his niece taking a shower.

"I need to see your body," he told her. "I'm sure it's quite nice, a pretty form in the buff; but you must get used to being naked, since that is how we will work together."

"I see," said Kathleen, and she casually, mechanically removed her clothes, panties and bra and stood in front of Edward, looking down at the floor, her hands in front of her crotch, goose bumps forming on her skin.

"Let me see your cunny," he said, "let me see that thick bush."

She removed her hands.

"Nice," he said, nodding, "very nice."

"Thank you," she said softly.

"Turn around and let me see your arse."

She did so.

"Nice. Now reach around and spread your cheeks, I want to see that shit hole."

She did so.

"Nice. Not a virgin in your poop chute, it seems."

Kathleen started to get wet.

Her nipples were hard.

Thinking about that night at the frat house party was getting her excited.

She liked what she was feeling…however alien and odd it all was.

"Turn around, pretty girl, and look at me."

She did so.

"Look at me."

Kathleen's eyes met his.

"You're not just a pretty girl," he said, "you're one sexy bird."

She smiled.

"Your nipples are hard, and I know it's just not the draft."

She stared at him.

"You like this," he said.

"Yes," she said.

"I want you to lie down on the couch over there," he said, "and masturbate for me."

She felt flush.

"It's what you'll be doing, and you need to practice."

"I *know* how to jill-off," she said.

He laughed and said: "'Jill-off,' I like that. Okay, show me."

She moved to the living room couch. It was white, it was big, and it was very comfortable—softer than her bed. She could just fall asleep on it.

"Keep your eyes open," Edward told her, "look at me, look at the ceiling, look at your feet, or look at me, but don't close your eyes. When you do it at the gallery, your eyes will be open, you will look at the people looking at you and you will make yourself come. You *can* make yourself come, can't you?"

"Of course I can," she said, fingering her clit.

"Go to town, baby," he said, "slip a couple fingers into that hairy little twat...."

She did this.

She looked at the ceiling and then she looked at him.

He was standing far away, observing, touching himself between the legs, squeezing the penis he had inside his pants.

"Do it," he said, moving closer.

She was rubbing her pussy hard, her pussy was dripping wet, and she came...and came again....

She was breathing hard...

"Oh fuck," and she made herself come a third time.

"Good, good, I bloody knew you had it in you," Edward Kaff said.

He was stroking her hair. He was sitting next to her. He touched her neck, her tits, her belly.

"You have nice skin, nice sweat," he said, "it smells sweet...it smells so...what's the word I'm looking for... feminine."

She smiled.

"You will do this to yourself, at the show, and then I will come to you like this, I will touch you like this, and I will do this," and he reached down and gave her a kiss. It was just a peck. He gave her another kiss, his tongue in her mouth. They kissed and he reached down and slid a finger into her....

"Okay?" he said.

"Okay," she said.

"I'm going to eat your pussy now," he said.

"That sounds...okay," she said.

"I'm very good at it," Kaff said, and this was no boast. When he got between her legs, and licked her pussy and her asshole for half an hour, she came three times. No boast at all. The man knew what to do with his tongue and two fingers.

He stood up and took his pants off. His cock stood up straight, was long and thick and veined. She said she wanted to suck on it but he told her that wasn't necessary; he told her it was time to fuck. "I'm going to fuck that cunny of yours for a very long time," he said, "and you're going to love it."

V.

Did she love it? Well, she enjoyed it—she got off—the old man was a great fuck, and let's face it: he was probably the best fuck she'd ever had. He kept going and going and she wondered how he was able to do that, what this "Tantric" stuff was all about. Maybe it was Viagra®. But he fucked her for a good three hours and after her twentieth orgasm, she stopped counting. They did take a break, when they drank some water and moved from the couch to the upstairs bedroom.

"Suck my cock now," he said, and she did, tasting the strong taste of her cunt juice all over that fat dick.

And then he came.

He came a lot.

He came so much she coughed, almost choked on all that semen going into her mouth and down her throat.

"Oh, oh," she said, spitting the stuff out.

"Yeah," he said, touching her hair.

"That's a lot."

"Lick it up."

She licked some of the sperm off the bed sheets and his flesh. He scooped a glob of it onto a finger and inserted the finger in her mouth and she sucked on his finger until all the semen was gone from it.

"Wow," she said.

"Did you have a good time?" Kaff asked her.

Kathleen admitted that she did.

"Good."

"Did you?" she asked him.

He said: "I always enjoy fucking women…especially young women like you."

"I bet you do," she said and smiled.

"So…I think we should rehearse this at least two or three more times before the show."

"Yeah," said Kathleen, "me too."

VI.

Kathleen went home that night feeling freshly, wonderfully fucked and even a little bit sore. She couldn't help herself and she masturbated, thinking of Kaff and his man meat and his impressive stamina. In the morning, she wanted to see him again, she wanted to "rehearse."

She went to the bank and deposited the check.

Her pussy was wounded so she knew she'd have to wait a day or two before more action. She didn't want to call him; she didn't want to appear over-anxious, eager, or horny—this whole matter was wrong, illicit, odd, not the sort of thing normal people engaged in when it came to sex, money, and the refuge of art.

She paid all her bills, paid rent for two months in advance, bought a lot of groceries and rented some movies to watch.

Three days later, Kaff called.

"You should come over," he said.

"Okay," Kathleen said.

VII.

And who was Edward Kaff? He was born not long after World War II, his father came home from the war (where he saw no action, he was a supply clerk) and married a girl he saw walking down the street one day. She was as pretty as sunshine. "Sweet one, some day I will marry you," the father said, and the mother said: "What's stopping you today, handsome?" They were wed a month later. Edward Kaff came along a year or so after that. He had an okay childhood, as far as childhoods go; nothing major happened until he was nineteen was his father shot himself in the head, in shame and fear, after his mother ran away with a woman. "My mom, the lesbian," mused Kaff; he never saw her again after that. He didn't even know if she knew her husband committed suicide. These are things that made Kaff a very cynical and angry young man. So he joined the Royal Marines and was shipped off to Northern Ireland to help keep the peace. He took some shrapnel in his leg from a poorly-made bomb that exploded 100 feet away from him. In the hospital, he befriended another soldier, Lance Williams. Williams had a semi-famous father who wrote pulp novels in the 1940s, a lot of science-fiction, mysteries, true confession, soft-core erotica, you name it, the man did it. The pulp days were over but Lance's dad, Luke, was writing the occasional space yarn or private dick tale under pen names as well as publishing some low-grade skin magazines out of a small office in Liverpool. "I'm going to go work for him, and so should you," Lance said. Kaff figured what the hell, why not, it wasn't like he had anything better to do with his life. Instead of working there, Kaff became an investor; he had some money in the bank left over by his father and this girly magazine business looked like it had potential—if nothing else, it provided an atmosphere for him to score plenty of pussy. Girls—beautiful, pretty, so-so and ugly—waltzed in every day wanting money for their nude shots, ideas in their silly heads that this one day might lead to Hollywood and some kind of stardom on the screen. They were all hippy chick of course; at first Kaff didn't care much for this drug-and-sex culture, mainly because they all seemed to hate soldiers…but what did it matter if he fucked them? So he fucked them, and he smoked pot with them, and he went to orgies and did a lot of acid and let his hair grow long and started wearing bell-bottom jeans and beads and granny glasses and saying the usual shit like, "heavy, man" and "I can grok that." He read Richard Brautigan and Jack Kerouac and Robert Heinlein and Kurt Vonnegut. What he did around the office was dubious; the outfit was called The Beck Consulting Group but that was just a shell to keep the cops away; they were putting out half a dozen girly magazines with revolving names like *Twat* and *Public Pubic* and *Beach Gal*, etc. What Kaff mostly did was interview potential models, take some photos, and fuck them. Lance Williams was doing editorial work, and dealing with distributors, while his father also did editorial and a lot of the writing, using up to twenty pen names. Luke had an idea about starting a line of soft-core sleaze novels—the genre was hot, others were making money off it, and Luke knew plenty of starving sci-fi and hardboiled detective writers who could churn these things out. Kaff figured why not, and took the money he'd made so far and re-invested it into this paperback line, dubbed

Moonlight in Lace Editions. Moonlight started with six ti-
tles a month and graduated to twenty. They paid the writers $1,000 a pop, no royalties, and sold an average of
100,000 each, pocketing the profits. The more books they
published, the more money they made. Kaff sat down and
penned one himself. It was awful, but it sold. It was a lesbian novel called *Housewives of Sin*, and he imagined his
mother the whole time he sat behind the typewriter. It was
a grueling, two-month task that he had the occasional
hippy chick fuck bunny sit behind the typewriter (naked,
of course) and write some scenes. "I *love* eating pussy,"
one would say, and Kaff would say, "Go write about it."
Anyway, they moved this operation out to San Diego—
better real estate, better weather, and no more cops coming
around looking for handouts. Once in San Diego, they
published more books and magazines and made more
money. They became millionaires. Kaff invested his
money to make more money to insure he would grow old
in comfort. He knew this business would never last. Eventually they sold the business off . Kaff traveled around
Europe for a while, enjoying his money, and moved three
years later to Los Angeles, thinking about getting into
Hollywood. He hated the Hollywood people; he tried writing screenplays but was no good at that. He knew there
was some kind of art in him so he began to paint, and
painting was something he knew he was good at. He returned to England. He had gallery showings; people
bought his stuff. He sculpted and did pottery. He began to
write poetry. He went back to America in the 1980s and
traveled a lot with a young girl he met (there were so many
of them). Women! Oh there were many women, many
women, and he learned a lot about fucking, about love-
making, about how to keep his cock hard for hours: those
ancient techniques. Yes, lots of women, but he was never
serious with them; he never married or fell in love; when a
woman became too close, he sent them on their way, damn

the tears! Back to Queen and country he went, broken hearts behind him. No, Edward Kaff never knew love, until he met Kathleen. How absurd, yes! But it happened. And we know how it happened: one day Edward Kaff was nearing his sixtieth birthday and all his art crowd friends in London wanted to throw him a shindig/birthday party at a gallery. Kaff thought about his wild sexual days in the 1970s, recalling a party he was at where three women masturbated as a show for all the attendees. How marvelous would that be? Kaff was going to hire a call girl to do this, until one day he was looking at some classifieds and saw Kathleen's ad.

VIII.

And so the big night finally came. "Are you ready?" Kaff asked Kathleen and she said: "As ready as I'll ever be."

"Then let's put on a show they'll never forget," said Kaff, giving her a light kiss on the cheek.

The gallery was located central London on Charing Cross Road. It was a big place with three levels and on every wall was a painting by none other than Edward Kaff himself. Kathleen didn't know much about art, but what she saw seemed okay—a lot of it was violent and sexual and, well, weird. Everyone attending looked rich and cultured; there were about 100 people and they were well-dressed, of all ages, and mingled about, drinking imported champagne and talking and laughing and looking at each other and, Kathleen assumed, gossiping. She was glad she didn't have to be around them; they were from a different world and they weren't the kind of people she would ever want to know. She was here to do a job and get the rest of her quid. So: she entered the gallery completely naked, holding a bag of assorted sex toys. Needless to say, without a doubt, and completely to Edward Kaff's plan, all chatter stopped, jaws dropped, eyes widened as Kathleen made her way though the people in the splendor of her skin.

"Ladies and gentlemen," announced Kaff, wearing a tuxedo and looking rather dapper, "may I present to you— *my slut!*"

No one knew what to make of this.

Kathleen walked over to a large beanbag that was placed in the center of the gallery. She lied on her back, spread her legs, closed her eyes, and went to work with her hand.

She could feel all the eyes on her, the heat of bodies closing in, the warmth of the lights…mumbles, confusion, fascination, one woman saying, "She has a small and pretty pussy."

"Fear not!" said Kaff, "for this is all part of the show. This young trollop, this lover of mine, this luscious piece of girl meat, this comely little whore who loves to diddle—*she is my new canvas, my finest work of art, my erotic masterpiece!*"

Hearing his voice…doing this…the people around her…the excitement of the strange…it made Kathleen come, and she was quite vocal about it.

Scattered applause.

"You see," said Kaff, "magnificent!"

She reached into the bag and took out the first sex toy—a small dildo.…

She peeked through her eyelids: so many faces and eyes watching her with blasé interest.…

"And now," said Kaff, "I shall read a very long poem. If you get bored, have a drink, have a finger food, watch the girl jill-off…it is all part of the show."

He read his poem, which took about an hour. She half-listened to it, paying more attention to her pussy and making herself come, going from the small dildo to the bigger one and to an even bigger one, as well as a butt-plug…

fucking herself with the rubber cocks as Kaff read his words that were filled with images of Europe and travel and vampires and music and Russia. What it all meant, she had no idea. She was no longer concerned with the people watching her...it didn't take long for most of them to become bored and go back to mingling, whispering, and drinking....

When Kaff was done reading, he went to her, joined her, touched her, kissed her, put his mouth to her vagina...

"More avant-garde theater, Eddy?" someone asked with an appropriate amount of sarcasm.

"You haven't seen nothing yet," he replied.

He undressed, and began to fuck her....

IX.

...and fucked and fucked for many hours like planned and promised and practiced. Most people got bored and left.

Then it was over.

"And so my latest art installation ends," said Kaff.

X.

"Here is your money," he said, handing her the second check.

She didn't look at it.

"Where will you go from here?" he asked.

"Your home," she said. "I would like...."

He said, "I would like that too," and that's what they did.

KARIN

It's night—the middle of summer—August—in a place where the summers last deep into September, creep into October, trickle into November. It's sweltering, tonight in a club where we go because the nights are too hot to sleep, too hot to dream. Here on the evening when I meet Justine.

The walls are tiled green like a high-school gym. The mattress on the floor in the middle of the next room is covered in a bloody plush, like velveteen. The sheets are emerald polyester. The club, where we go because there's nowhere else to go, where we go to escape the sun-baked streets, is a haphazard mess of textures, the scent of sweaty bodies juxtaposed with hair oil and wheatgrass.

When I meet Justine.

She is sitting at the bar doing shots of grenadine. I spot her. I approach. I conjure a line or two. Blah, blah. Skip to the sex scene:

I lick the delicate curls of her cunt with a nervous tongue. Swirling betwixt the swirls. She whinnies softly. I need to please her. Need to badly. My sex organs are engorged with the blood that mounts in her thighs. My senses are inflamed with the pounding acid of her juices. We are thick, clasped together mouth to cunt. Her flesh shivers. Cut to the inciting incident

The night is thick with thunder. She says she has something to show me. I don't know what she means. "Show me, slut."

The showing involves eating a weird, dried plant; and the plant doesn't taste very good. I vomit into the sickly green tile wall of the club, into the wall that is sealed white without a chink.

This is how the story begins:

* * * * * * *

Alone, together, sequestered in a small room like prisoners in a cell, she ravages my asshole. Justine has no interest in my cunt, which I find odd for a girl like her. All she wants to do is play with my ass—wants to torture it, hurt it, please it, make me go places I didn't know my ass could go. She shoves her fingers in, shoves her whole hand in—a hand well-greased with lube. She says: "Karin, Karin, how far do you want me to go?" I want her in deep. Her hand goes in *deep*. She has my wrists tied, I can't stop her. Fist-fucking my asshole is not enough. My cunt wants her attention, but she's not going to do this. She has a huge and thick black dildo. She waves it in my face and I can smell its rubber shell. She says, "Just pretend a black dude with this really big dick is fucking you," but it's no use telling her that I am tired of black dudes fucking me with their big dicks and Justine sticks the dildo in, she shoves it deep, she makes me hurt, she makes me shit and bleed, she pulls it out and says I should see how wide and round my ass is, but I know oh I know, I have seen my ass stretched to its limits.

The music is loud and my head pounds.

"Now I'll lick your cunt," she says.

"Oh," I say.

JOLENE

The nice thing about living near the beach in Southern California is that, when summer arrives, the clothes on women's skin scatter like cockroaches in neon light.

A walk down the boardwalk guaranteed a view of many fine, round asses split in two by thong bikinis; up and down any block and there were plenty of miniskirts, hot pants, tube tops, and see-through blouses.

I noticed this even more after my girlfriend moved out of the apartment; summer was here and I'd been a hermit, and celibate, just a little too long.

The house next to my apartment building threw parties every other weekend. Three young women lived there. The day before a party, one of them would knock on all the apartments and say, "We just want to let you know we're having a party so if we're too loud, please don't call the cops, just let us know. And you're invited to come over and hang if you want."

"Maybe I will," I said, the next time one of the women showed up at the door. She had long, wavy brunette hair and wore a flower-print dress, and she was braless. Her nipples were hard, the way nipples get. I found myself staring at them. She noticed. She raised a brow. She didn't seem to mind.

"Yeah," she said, "you should." She rolled her eyes. Still, I went. I didn't care that most of the people at the party were five, ten years younger than me. I just wanted to drink and mingle. That's when I met Allison.

* * * * * * *

Allison was petite, pale, with dark makeup, a platinum blonde with streaks of green and blue in that hair. She wore a lacy black dress that cut off just above her knees. She looked like she'd be more at home at a smoky Goth dance club than at this party. I felt the same way, which is how we started talking.

"I really don't know anyone," she said.

"Neither do I," I said.

We both shrugged and had some beer and talked, and she said she wished there were some good drugs here. People were smoking joints but she wasn't into pot. I mentioned that I had an ounce of magic mushrooms and two grams of coke at home; the stuff had been sitting around for months because I hadn't had the opportunity or desire to party.

"Shrooms!" she said, and: "Blow! My two most favorite things in the world, except for dick."

We went back to my apartment, and what can I say about what happened next? We got high and she seemed to be happy to be high and we fooled around. Didn't take us long to go from heavy kissing and grabbing to my bedroom and getting naked and some crazy fucking and sucking in the hot and sticky and almost gloomy summer night. She was a screamer. I wondered if people at the party next door could hear her. I knew my neighbors probably did and I didn't care. I had a fantasy of my ex-girlfriend coming by to check on me, peering through the bedroom window and seeing me sweat it out with this beautiful woman. That idea made me come hard, and profusely.

"Well," my quickie said, pulling her panties up, "I have to get back to the party. My boyfriend is probably wondering where I am."

"Boyfriend?"

"Okay, he's my husband."

"Husband," I said.

"Don't worry," she said, "he doesn't care."

"I see," I said, and tried to smile.

"You coming back to the party?"

"Maybe later."

She reached down and gave me a quick kiss and said, "Thanks," and left.

I did want to go back—there wasn't anything to do in an apartment that still had her smell and I was curious about this husband who didn't care; I wondered what he looked like and if she let him fuck around too.

I fell asleep.

Around 3 A.M., I heard some voices, laughter, and a woman say: "Okay, I'll pull a train with you guys, sounds like fun."

Sounded like they were outside my window, but they were in one of the bedrooms of the house next door. I guess the party was still going on, in a fashion. I looked out my window. It was dark in my bedroom and dark outside, except for half a moon in the sky, and the light was on and the blinds up in the bedroom where the voices were coming from. I saw one of the female roommates—she was Korean and tall, and she was taking her bra off. There were four guys in the room watching her, encouraging her, and looking at each other and grinning and high-fiving one another. They moved around the room, each guy making out with her for half a minute, then she would do the next. One of them slapped her on the ass. I saw that she had shaved her dark pubes to a slim Mohawk. She unzipped one guy's pants, took his dick out, and got on her knees. I couldn't see anything, except for a bobbing head of dark hair, until she brushed her hair back for the next guy who stood in front of her with his cock out, ready to suck.

This was too much. I thought for a moment I was

dreaming. This was too good. I thought about this neighbor, whose name I now remembered was Jolene, and how I'd seen her around—next door, sure, but riding her bike, or at the store, or down at the beach in a green bikini, always that green bikini that barely covered her tits or her ass. She always ignored me, as if she didn't know I was her neighbor; she did the same when I was at the party earlier.

I observed her get on the bed, but I couldn't see her body. I saw her legs being lifted as one of the guys fucked her. He fucked her for five minutes, the other three watching, and when he was done, another guy took position.

I had to get in on this action.

I had to see this closer.

I had to be there.

I went back to the house. The door was open. There were still some people there, lounging around, drunk or high or asleep. I made my way to Jolene's bedroom. She was moaning, saying, "Yes, yes, fuck me, baby, fuck me good," and all the usual words a woman utters when she's engaged in a gang bang.

Yes, a gang bang it was. The third guy was now doing her up the ass and there were three more men in the room, watching…and waiting.

Jolene turned her head and looked at the men looking at her. She squinted at me. She said, "Who are you? Do I know you? You look familiar."

I was going to leave when some guy said, "Hey, he's just in line, like the rest of us. But you'll fuck him, won't you, you dirty slut?"

"Yeah, yeah," she said as the guy in her asshole came. "I'll fuck every one of you, I'll fuck every guy in the world if I have to."

"And you *would*!" another guy said and chuckled, softly.

"I would," Jolene said, staring at me.

I stood there and watched her get fucked by two other guys, as five more came into the room, holding drinks, smiling.

It was getting crowded in the bedroom, and hot. Hot from the bodies, the weather, the rising sun, the sexual energy. I was sweating a lot and not even doing anything. Jolene was covered in sweat, and it looked like she was crying too, but she kept telling the next guy, "Stick it in whatever hole you want," and they did.

My turn was coming up at some point, but I didn't take it. I didn't want to be here. I could barely breathe in the room; it was so filled with the smell of pussy, ass, semen, perspiration, and desire.

I backed away.

I left the bedroom.

I left the house.

I went home.

* * * * * * *

I watched the rest from my bedroom window, my view into her bedroom, as Jolene got fucked until long after sunrise. Twice, I jacked off, thinking about what it was like. The fantasy was better than the real, nasty thing.

* * * * * * *

Ten days later, a Saturday, and I was down at the beach. The beach was crowded because it was a holiday weekend. There were bodies all over the sand getting tanned and surfers riding the summer waves. I was there to look at women and darken my skin.

I saw Jolene. I hadn't seen her around since the night of the party. I saw her in that green bikini, lying on her stomach, a small radio by her ear. The radio was playing a song by Depeche Mode, something old and classic from the 1980s that made me feel nostalgic. I almost went up to her, to say, "Hi neighbor," but that felt stupid, and I had nothing, really, to say to the woman.

I laid my towel down about a hundred feet away from her, though. At one point I noticed her looking at me.

As I was leaving the beach and walking home, she came up behind me. She was wearing a small white dress over her bikini.

"Hey, you," Jolene said.

"Hey."

"I know you."

"We're neighbors," I said.

"I mean" she said, but didn't go on. She looked angry.

"What's wrong?" I asked.

"I need a drink. A beer. Something. Feel like one?"

"Always."

"There are many bars up that block," she said, pointing and nodding.

"I've been to them all," I said.

"I think I have too," she said, putting on a pair of big black sunglasses.

We went into one of the bars that had a lot of surf-boards leaning against the wall and shared a pitcher of Heineken. Nothing like drinking Heineken on a bright, sunny day, while sitting next to a half-naked, hot slut.

"Okay," Jolene said, "you were in my bedroom the other night."

"You remember."

"What? I wasn't drunk or high. I was *horny*."

"Do you do that sort of thing often?"

"Pull a train?"

"Yeah."

"Only once, in college. It was fun. The other night was fun. So the big question is: why didn't you take a turn? Huh?" She hit me on the arm. "Tell me, neighbor, why didn't you fuck me?"

"I don't know."

"What kind of answer is that?"

"I don't know."

"You didn't *want* to?"

"To?"

"Take a turn."

"I wanted to very much," I said.

"So-o-o," she said.

"I felt uncomfortable," I told her.

"Why?"

"I don't know."

"If you say those three words again I'll sock you in the teeth and you'll have no teeth and look like a redneck trailer park hick, motherfucker."

She was serious.

"You're a violent one," I said.

"I can be," she said. "Now answer me."

"I've never been involved in a gang bang."

"Did you ever think you probably insulted me?" Jolene asked, getting in my face so I could smell the beer on her breath and the suntan lotion on her skin. "That I felt ugly, unwanted, dirty, slutty, worthless, because you wouldn't fuck me?"

"You had plenty of other guys to do that."

"Not the point, buddy!" she said, pointing a finger at my face. "Not the point!"

We sat there and drank beer in silence.

"Now I'm all worked up," she said.

"Yeah."

"You still want to fuck me?"

"Yeah."

"So let's get out of here and take care of business."

"Okay."

* * * * * * *

We didn't waste time at my apartment; went straight to the bedroom. She undressed on the way and was naked by the time we lay down. Her skin tasted like sweat, lotion, and the beach. She took me in her mouth and I came just a little too fast, but she didn't mind. She grabbed my head and said, "Get down there," pushing me into her crotch. Briefly, only briefly, did I think about all those guys who'd been in her pussy the other night, before I began licking and sucking at said pussy. Then I started to think about the gang bang as I slipped two fingers in her and made her come. I made her come a second time, and the more I thought about the other men, the more excited I got, and I was hard, and I yanked myself up and made my way inside her and she said, "Yeah, fuck me like that," or something like that, I wasn't really paying attention.

* * * * * * *

Jolene wanted to get more beer. We walked two blocks down to a dive bar called the Tilted Stick. It was getting dark out. We sat at the counter and ordered pints of a beer called Chronic. "Yeah, me gots the Chronic," Jolene said gleefully; we raised our pint glasses and toasted to a good fuck.

"There's nothing like a good fuck," she said, "a nice hard fuck."

I concurred.

There was a blonde in a miniskirt next to me. She was tipsy and glassy-eyed. She tapped me on the shoulder and said, "You see that line?"

She was pointing to a line in the wood of the bar counter.

"Yeah," I said.

"You keep leaning into me," she said, "so let's say that this line shows where your side is, and where my side is. So don't cross the line, okay? What do you think about that?"

"I think you're drunk," I told her, "and obnoxious."

"You what?"

"You heard me."

Jolene watched with interest.

"I'm not obnoxious," the blonde in the miniskirt said. "Drunk, sure, but I'm not *mean*. Do you think I'm *mean*?" She used her fingers to make quotes in the air.

I said, "Yes."

"I was just *kidding*. I was *flirting*. You're cute. It was a joke. Jeez."

"Still," I said, turning back to Jolene.

"What's up?" asked Jolene.

"This drunk chick is giving me shit," I said.

"Hey!" the blonde said. "I said I was kidding." She grabbed me and spun me around on my barstool and got into my face. She smelled like tequila. "Don't you call me an obnoxious drunk! Who the hell do you think you are?!"

Jolene pushed the blonde away and got in between.

"What the" said the blonde.

"You want to fight, bitch?" Jolene said. "Let's rock and roll, bitch."

The blonde just stared at Jolene as if she was Godzilla.

Imagine that—two hot women ready to fight over ugly ol' me.

The blonde backed off, told her friends, "Let's go," and left the bar.

I could feel the energy coming off Jolene's body, like a fully charged battery. She turned and grabbed my head and gave me a big wet, Chronic-flavored kiss.

"Thanks," I said.

"That was *hot*," she said.

"It was something wonderful, all right."

"I'm wet," she whispered. "Let's go back to your place and fuck like fuckers."

And we went back to my place and fucked like

HOW TO HAVE AN AFFAIR, BY HEMMINGSON

fuckers.

NATALIE

I was at Barry's place; we were kicking back and watching some Hong Kong action movies he'd ordered over the Internet. His phone rang. "Yeah, yeah, sure, okay," Barry said and put the phone down. "Natalie's coming over," he said.

I was very interested.

"Oh really," I said.

"Really," he said, and yawned.

I'd wanted to fuck Natalie for several months now. But she always eluded the right time and the right moves. She said she had a boyfriend, but the boyfriend was hardly ever around...he was a freelance roadie and there were always bands that needed him to go on the road and keep their instruments in tune and the tubes up-to-date in the amplifiers, among the other things roadies did.

"She sounds whacked," Barry said.

"Good," I said.

"She drives me up the wall sometimes," he said.

"She needs to get rid of that boyfriend," I said.

"Or he needs to get rid of her," Barry said.

Natalie arrived fifteen minutes later. She was sweaty, smelled like tequila. "Brisk walk," she said, giggling, giving us both a hug and a kiss on the cheek.

"Nice outfit, Natalie," I said.

She was wearing a white cotton tank top and tight white shorts with the word LOOK on her ass. Her ass was hanging out of the shorts. She wasn't wearing a bra, the cotton top was see-through, especially with that film of sweat....

I imagined Natalie walking the seven blocks from her apartment, that ass swaying, the sweat forming on her skin...and cars honking her. "Cars always honk at me," she'd said more than once.

"What?" she said.

"I like your jogging gear," I said.

"You like?" she said. "I *bet* you do," she said, looking over her shoulder and smiling at me.

"Oh, I do," said I.

"Pervert," said she.

"And what's so perverted about looking?"

*"Every*thing," she said, walking away, going: "Barry, what do you got to drink around here?"

"There's that bottle of Chivas you left last time," Barry said.

"Yum."

"You want to drink more?" he said.

"Glug, glug," Natalie said, holding her head up, mouth open, and pointing a thumb down.

"You're drunk already," Barry said.

"I had a few," she said. "Hey, I'm young, I can drink gallons," she said.

She was twenty-five. Barry was thirty. I was thirty-three.

She made us all a drink.

"Party away, boys," she said. "Hey, what were you two doing? Watching pornos and jerking off?"

"Kung fu movies," Barry said.

Natalie rolled her eyes. "You and your funny movies, kid."

Somehow we wound up in Barry's bedroom. Natalie finished her drink and was lying on the bed, on her stomach. I was sitting next to her, thinking about the right kind of move to make on the girl. Barry stood, looking annoyed, playing with his drink.

"I must be crazy," Natalie said.

"Yes," Barry said, "you are."

"I must be crazy," she said, "being here with you two like this. As far as I know, you both might kill me."

"Funny," Barry said. "Look at me: ha, ha."

"Ha?"

"Ha."

He seemed uncomfortable.

Natalie turned her head to look at me and said, "Maybe just you. *You*, you might just slice up my flesh and filet me."

"You'd like that," Barry said, "I think."

"You know, I might," she said.

"Filet your ass?" I said, and gave her ass a soft smack.

"Mmm," Natalie went, wiggling her butt.

I smacked it again.

"Oh," she said, "you're bad. Will you filet me now?"

"I wouldn't filet this ass," I said, "I'd just fuck it."

"Promises, promises," she mumbled.

I hit her ass, hard.

She wiggled and moaned.

"Bad Natalie," I said.

"I'm very bad," she said, "I need a good spanking."

I smacked both her cheeks a few times.

"I need to get hand to flesh," I said, noticing a few brown pubic hairs sticking out of her shorts.

Natalie lifted herself up as I pulled her shorts down to her ankles...one ankle anyway.

"No undies," I said, "bad Natalie."

"I'm a bad girl, Big Daddy," she said.

I gave her a few more tender slaps, then slid a finger into her cunt.

"Okay, guys," Barry said, "I'll leave you two alone."

"No, stay," Natalie said.

"I'll just be out here," Barry said, stuttering.

I moved a finger into Natalie's asshole.

"You're the bad, bad, bad boy," she said.

I leaned down and kissed her left cheek, slightly red from my touch.

"Was that a promise or a threat?" she asked me.

"What?"

"That you'd fuck my ass rather than filet it."

"Why don't I do both?"

"I have a boyfriend...."

"Does that matter now?"

"I mean, it's okay if you fuck my ass, but not my pussy."

"Because of your boyfriend?"

"Yeah."

That didn't make sense, but I didn't care. I managed a second finger into her asshole.

"You do have a condom, I hope," she said.

"That I have. But hang on. Don't go anywhere."

"I'm right here, Big Daddy."

"Don't call me that," I said.

"Yessir."

I went to the living room. Barry was watching TV. "Hey," I said.

"Hey," he said.

"Do you have any lube? K-Y?"

"There's some Vaseline in the bathroom. Why?"

"Why do you think?"

"Are you really going to fuck her?" Barry asked.

"Finally, yes. Don't you want to?"

"Not really."

"You can go first if you want."

Barry sat up. "Look," he said, "have fun. I'm going for a walk. How long do you need?"

"Don't know."

"I'll be back in an hour," he said, and left.

I returned to the bedroom with the bottle of Vaseline. Natalie was still on the bed, a pillow under her hips now. She was playing with her clit.

"I made myself come when you were gone, dude," she said.

I hovered above her, my pants down, the rubber on my cock. I started to apply the Vaseline to her.

"Where's Barry?" she asked.

"He left."

"Why?"

"He needed a stroll."

"Does he hate me?"

"No."

"I wish he was here."

"Me too."

I fucked Natalie for fifteen minutes, smacking her little butt cheeks now and then. "Hit me harder," she said, and I did. By the time I came her rear end was bright red.

I lay down next to her.

"Everything you hoped for?" she said.

I smiled.

"I see how you always look at me," she said.

"It's the way you dress."

"How do I dress? Like a whore?"

"Like you want to get fucked."

"I always want to get fucked," she said, "I just don't get fucked by the right men."

"What do you mean?"

"I wish Barry was here," she said, "he could fuck me next."

"He's not here."

"No, I guess he is not. So you'll have to fuck me again, if you want to."

"I want to," I said.

"You can fuck my pussy this time. My ass is sore, you fucked that too hard and it'll be sore for a week."

She giggled.
I slapped her one across the two cheeks.
She turned over on her back.
"Pussy next," she said, "I want it in the pussy."
"What about your boyfriend?" I asked.
She said, "The hell with him."

* * * * * * *

I was watching the rest of the interrupted Hong Kong flick when Barry returned, two hours later.
"There you are," I said.
"Where is she?" he said.
"Asleep."
"Passed out, you mean."
I shrugged.
Barry sat down. "So you fucked her?"
"Three times."
"Everything you hoped for?"
I laughed. "She said the same thing."
"Whatever," he said.
"What? Why don't you want her? She wants you to fuck her."
"I know. But I don't want to."
"Why? She's gorgeous, hot, sexy…."
"I work with her, we work at the same goddamn place…."
"So?"
"One," he said, "I don't mess with co-workers. It's bad…."
"So?"
"Two, she had a boyfriend."
"So?"
"Three, she's nuts."
"Ahhh," I said, waving a hand.

"Really," Barry said, "something isn't right in that girl's head."

* * * * * * *

The next day, Natalie called me while I was jerking off, thinking about her.

"Hey," she said.

"Speak of the devil," I said.

"What's that?"

"How are you?"

"Sober," she said. "Can I come over? We need to talk."

"We can talk on the phone,"

"I want to talk face to face," she said, serious.

"Okay," I said.

She knocked on my door half an hour later. She was wearing faded jeans and a purple tank top, again no bra. Hard dark nipples, etc. Hair pulled back in a ponytail. Bright lipstick.

"Drink?" I said. "I have vodka…."

"Tempting," she said, "but no."

We sat down on the couch, distance between us.

"Look," she said, "yesterday."

"Yeah."

"I was really drunk."

"I know."

"You took advantage of me."

"No I didn't."

"Okay, you didn't."

"So," I said.

"So I was upset about something, that's why I got drunk, and I didn't want to be alone. So I called Barry. I came over. And there you were…."

"Regrets?"

"I feel funny."

"Why?"

"I went to Barry's because I wanted Barry to fuck me."

"But not yours truly?" I said.

"Look," she said.

"Should I feel insulted?" I asked.

"Not at all," she said. "I like you."

"Well, that's good," I said with a smile.

"We're friends," she said, "and I don't have many friends, you know."

But my heart felt sad because I knew where she was going.

"You scare me a little," she said; "what I said about you cutting me up and making my meat into filet...."

"Oh come on," I said.

"I'm kidding," she said, but I knew she wasn't.

"It was nice," I said, "being inside you."

"I can see myself being in love with Barry," she said. "But he hates me," she said.

"No he doesn't," I said. "He cares about you."

"Like I was a stray cat," she said.

"The thing with Barry," I started to say.

"He's afraid of women," she said. "He likes his movies better," she said, "because movies aren't real."

"No," I said.

"It's because his last girlfriend tore his heart apart," she said.

"Yeah," I said.

"I could mend that heart."

"Do you really want him that much?" I asked.

"It's a fantasy," she said. "Look, my boyfriend can never know what happened between us."

"Okay."

"Well, I don't give a crap. I'm going to break up with him."

"Oh?"

"He's been fucking girls on the road, groupies and shit," she said. "Can you believe that? And I've been so good. Why should I be good? Tell me? Why?"

"You shouldn't," I said.

"No," she said, "I shouldn't."

I pushed the sadness out of my heart and filled the space with a lewd darkness.

"You're bad," I said.

"I am," she said.

"You're a wicked wench," I said, "a naughty slut."

"That's me, boy," she said.

"You should be treated as such."

"I should, shouldn't I?"

"Yes," I said, "and what you're going to do, slut, is lay across my lap right now, and I am going to give you what all bad girls who cheat on their boyfriends get."

"And what's that?"

"The spanking of their lives."

Natalie stood, took off her jeans and panties, and lay across my lap.

"You better hit me really hard," she said.

"I will," I said.

Later, as she got dressed, Natalie said, "This can never happen again, okay?"

"Okay," I said.

"Oh my ass is going to be so black and blue tomorrow," she said.

"I hope so," I said.

"This is a one time thing, okay?" she said, looking at the wall.

I nodded; after she left the sadness returned.

* * * * * * *

Three days later, she called before midnight.

"Sorry," she said. "Asleep?"

"I'm awake."

"I didn't know who to call."

"What's wrong?"

"Nothing's wrong."

"You're calling."

"I wanted to hear your voice," she said.

"I like the sound of your voice, too," I said.

"I broke up with my boyfriend," she said.

I wanted to say good.

"He didn't care," she said.

"Where are you?" I asked. I could hear the sound of cars.

"He doesn't know me," Natalie said. "He never whacked my ass like you do. I don't think Barry would either."

"Where are you?"

"A payphone, three blocks away."

"What are you doing?"

"Can I come over?"

"Of course," I said.

"Will you bend me over and spank me hard?" she said. "Will you tell me how much I'm a very bad, naughty little girl?"

"Of course," I said, "and then some."

"And this time, after you pound my ass raw," she said very softly, "I want you to make love to me."

MO

Crack the code. My digital sex life with Mo was fun, but for the most part, silly. I soon got tired of it; it was all right when you were bored and on the computer, but the novelty could only last for so long.

What are you doing right now? Mo IM'ed me.

Nothing, I wrote back. *Just sitting here.*

Why don't you come over?

Where do you live?

She gave me her address. I was leery at first, wondering if I was being set up. For all I knew, Mo could be a guy. She did tell me she was Asian, nineteen, and that people said she was pretty. What the hell, I believed her, and went to her place.

She was fortunate to be living in the apartments and not the dorms, for an undergraduate, but still she shared the place with two other young women (whom I had not met yet). Mo greeted me in a long white terry-cloth robe. Like most kids at the university, she didn't get out of bed until afternoon. She was an exquisite young woman, and part of my delight was that she was indeed a young woman, and real at that. She was Asian, as she had said, and had dark eyes, brown skin, and long straight black hair. She was tall and slender and she smiled at me at the door and said, "Hello," and let me in. "So," she said, "you're WmGibson."

"WmGibson" was the screen name I used on line—a bad one at that, all the cyberpunk connotations laid right out.

"Actually," I said, "my name is Nick."

"You said."

"I did?"

"Yeah."

"Nicky," I said.

"I like 'WmGibson,'" Mo said.

The apartment smelled of young women and looked like they lived there. I felt awkward, being older than Mo. I knew that many of the graduate students who were teaching assistants slept with their freshmen students—it was all par for the course. But I wasn't a T.A., and Mo wasn't one of my students. I was getting ahead of myself, anyway—how did I know that something of a sexual nature was going to occur between Mo and me? Maybe she had just invited me over to be friendly?

Mo offered me something to drink, and I said milk would be nice. She laughed at that, and said, "Don't you want a beer?"

"Not now," I said.

"I have milk," she said.

She got me a glass of milk and she had a soda. We talked some; it was small talk. Her robe kept falling opening, giving me a glimpse of her cleavage, but each time she'd quickly close it. I was falling in lust. Mo never wiped away the sultry grin she maintained, and I couldn't read what was in her small dark eyes, often covered by strands of her jet-black hair. I detected something insidious. I didn't know if I should make a move or not.

"Let's get on line," she suggested, "and tell everyone you're here. That should stir up some gossip."

It didn't sound exciting to me, but I said, "Why not?" Mo lived to be online; she was a true William Gibson character in the flesh—bright, Asian, Net-savvy. I asked about her heritage, and she said her family had come from Korea.

She took me to her bedroom, one of three in the unit. It was small and cluttered, with a single bed, a desk, and a Macintosh computer. It smelled feminine. Clothes were strewn all over the floor—skirts, jeans, blouses, bras, panties.

She logged into one of the chatrooms we both frequented; sure enough, people we knew were there, both on-campus and all over the globe.

Guess who is here in my room? Mo typed. *WmGibson!* :^)

Some people said hello to me, some said they didn't believe it.

"Say hello," Mo said to me, getting up from her desk.

I sat at the desk. Mo perched on the edge of her bed, which was very close to the desk.

Hey everyone, I typed. *It is me, WmGibson, aka Nicky Bayless, and I am here with Mo.*

Answers were like so:

No way!

Kiss Mo!

Jerk!

It's Mo fooling again.

I felt silly typing, *No, it's really me.*

This is when Mo slipped her foot between my legs. First she guided her naked foot, with clean, well-clipped nails, up my leg, leaned back on the bed, and got her foot into my crotch. This wasn't an easy thing to do, as I had my torso half-turned in the chair. I turned some more.

She sprang up and came to me. She sat in my lap. She reached for the keyboard and typed: *Guess what I'm going? Rubbing WmGibson's cock and balls with my left foot!*

She added: *I'm now trying to stick my big toe up his asshole. His asshole is resistant, but my toe is getting in there.*

I laughed, and she laughed.

As the chatroom clamor went on, I touched Mo—her back, her neck, her breasts. She stood, and we embraced. She ran her fingers through my hair and it felt nice. I kissed her chest where the robe opened.

"I haven't showered in three days," she told me. "I must be gross."

"No," I said, though I could smell and taste her sweat.

I started to stand, to kiss her. She pushed me back down on the chair.

"I don't kiss," she said.

"What?"

"Anyone."

"Why?"

"I hate saliva," she said. "Mouths, tongues—yuck."

We continued to embrace and touch. I pulled at the sash of her robe.

She said, "What do you think you're doing, little boy?"

"I want to see your body," I said. "You won't let me kiss you, so let me see your body."

"Only for a second," she said.

She opened her robe, still in my arms, and revealed her young, beautiful frame. Medium-sized breasts with dark nipples, an "outie" belly button, a thick patch of black pubic hair. She then closed her robe and smiled and said, "*There,* you've seen it."

"Kiss me."

"No way."

I pulled her to me, my face pressing between her covered breasts. She continued to run her fingers through my hair.

"Play on the Net," she said. "I'm going to take a shower."

"Now?"

"I *need* a shower."

She left me there, at her desk, and went into the bathroom. I heard the water run. I logged her account off, and logged onto mine, getting back on the same chatroom channel.

Hey, someone named Nexus said, *are you really at Mo's place?*

Yes, I replied.

Coolio.

I was getting all the signals wrong. Mo was naked in the shower, I could see from my chair; I saw the hot water hitting her brown body, rolling down it. I logged off, got up, and went in.

"Is that you?" Mo said from the shower.

There was a lot of steam. I said, "Yes."

"It's about time," she said. "Get naked and join me."

I got naked and joined her.

We spent a good twenty minutes cleaning one another with a bar of soap, shampooing each other's hair, and touching each other's sex. I took every opportunity I could get to feel her body—her neck, her chest, her breasts, her stomach, her ass, her cunt. She let me finger her clit, but wouldn't let me slide my finger in; each time I tried, she said, "No, not yet." Not yet? And she still wouldn't kiss me on the lips; she allowed me to kiss other parts of her body, but not the lips. She took my hard cock in her hand, stroked it, and took it in both hands. I made myself not come. We got out of the shower and dried each other off. Naked, we went back to her bedroom. I pushed her toward the bed.

"I said I will not kiss you," she said.

"I know," I said, and put my mouth on her tits.

I reached for her cunt. She sat up. I lay on the bed, rubbed her back.

"You should know something," she said. "I'm a virgin."

"I've heard that before," I said, and stifled a sad…a very sad laugh.

"What?" she said, and just when I thought she would tell me I could fuck her in the ass, Mo said, "I swallow."

"What's that?"

"I can suck like a crazy machine," she said.

"Show me," I said.

"I want to show you," she said, and did. She went down on my cock. She wasted no time, and soon had the whole thing in her mouth. She cupped my balls in her hand, squeezing just a little too hard. After the whole shower bit, I was ready to explode, and explode I did, several huge spurts of semen, which she swallowed completely.

"Yum," she said. "Reminds me, I'm hungry. You want to go get something to eat?"

"I want to eat *you*," I said.

"Not now, later," she said. She stood, and went to her closet. "I need food. I don't want to eat on campus."

"There's plenty of places to go," I said.

"Okay," she said. "Don't watch me dress."

"I just like looking at you."

"I *don't* like people watching me dress. Go get your clothes on."

I went to the bathroom and retrieved my clothes, like a good boy.

* * * * * * *

We went to get pizza a few miles off campus. She ordered a beer and wasn't carded.

She leaned forward, voice low. "I can still taste your come in my mouth. The back of my mouth, really. You just pumped your come in my mouth and I don't know anything about you. Don't you think that's kinda weird, on my part?"

"I'm getting hard again."

"Good. I like guys who're always hard."

"Tell me about you," I said.

"I like sucking dick," she said. "I like to swallow. I could swallow all day."

"I'm twenty-eight," I said.

"Nice."

"Grad student."

"Nice."

"I write things."

"Nice."

"But you know all this."

"Yes."

"So what do you want to know?"

"Do you have a girlfriend?"

"No."

"Do you want me to be your girlfriend?"

"Yes."

"Will you marry me?"

"I don't know you."

"Will you *marry* me?"

"Yes," I said.

"Tonight?"

"We could drive to Vegas."

"Mo Bayless. Sounds funny."

"Let's do it," I said.

"I'd give up my virginity for the man who'd marry me."

"We can be in Vegas before midnight," I said.

She said, "Many guys wanna marry me."

"I bet."

"I have a lot of boyfriends."

"I bet," I said, and asked, "Do you swallow them all?"

She said, "Yes."

"Oh."

"I bet you have girlfriends."

"Women come and go in my life," I said. "Dark entries."

"And I'm just another," she said.

"Tell me about Maureen."

"Mo."

"Oh?"

"I hate 'Maureen.'"

"Mo."

"Mo has nowhere to go," she said, softly.

"What?"

She eyed me. "My parents would never approve of you."

"I'm too old."

"Too white."

"I see."

"I have to marry a nice Korean man"

"I could fake it," I said.

"Someday."

"But not today?"

"Today," she said, "I'd marry you."

"Let's do it."

"You just want my pussy."

"I want *you*."

"Are you still hard?"

"Very."

"I want to swallow you again," she said. "Maybe for dessert?"

"Let's eat fast."

"Behavioral science," Mo said.

"What?"

"My major. For now."

"How am *I* behaving?"

"Too nice," she said.

"What should I do, to not be so nice?"

"Grab me by the hair. Force me to suck your dick."

"Here?"

"Sure."

When we were done eating, and in my car, I grasped her hair, hard. I tried to kiss her.

"Don't kiss me," she said, a hand propped against my chest.

"Dammit," I said.

"Make me suck your dick. I have these elaborate fantasies that I'll tell you about someday."

I took my cock out, grabbed her head, and pushed her down on it. I closed my eyes, enjoying the sensation of her blow job. I came in her mouth the second time that night.

I took Mo home, and there I met her two roommates, both of whom had short hair and were nineteen or twenty, young.

"Just another guy," I said to Mo when we got into her room, referring to her roommates' looks.

"Do you care?"

"No," I said.

"Do you want your dick sucked more?"

"Yes," I said.

We undressed in the dark, and lay on the bed, where she took my cock back into her mouth. I wanted her, too; I told her this.

Mo said, "I'd like your face in my pussy."

I was quick to get between her legs. Now I had her cunt before me, the fresh smell of it, and I licked it. I spread it open. I couldn't admire, in the dark, what I knew must have been the beauty of a virgin twat, but I could taste it, and it was the sweetest cunt I've ever had on my tongue, my lips, my mouth. Mo squirmed with delight, and made enough loud sounds that I knew her roommates were getting an earful. I moved a finger to her opening, and was surprised she let me do this. I slid the finger in. Mo's body tensed all over, and began to shake. "That's it, Nicky," she said, "finger-fuck that kitty," and I did, sliding it in and out, my tongue pressed and lapping against her clit the whole time. Mo's shaking became almost frightening, but intriguing and fun at the same time; and she came with such a shrill cry I'm sure it echoed all across the campus.

I kissed her belly button, my lips wet with her sex. I moved up to kiss her mouth, but she looked away. I moved up still more, so that my cock was at her lips. She took it. My hands were against the wall by the bed, balancing my body, so that I was able to move my cock in and out of her mouth with the motion of my hips, fucking her pretty Asian face. Looking down, all I could see was the silhouette of her hair, and a slight whiteness of her eyes, as she was looking up at me. Mo's hands grabbed my ass, pulling me, making me fuck her mouth deeper. She squeezed and rubbed my ass, and one finger-nailed digit moved to touch my asshole. I was a piston, going in and out of her mouth, and soon I too let out a loud groan (maybe too loud, maybe wanting her roommates to hear) and came in Mo's mouth a third time that night.

I came in her mouth a fourth time a few hours later, waking up to her sucking me off. It took me a good while to get there that fourth time, but she didn't seem to mind, and I enjoyed every minute, every second.

It was awkward sleeping in that single bed with her; we had to be close and entwined. Sleeping with someone else, I usually like room. But it was nice. Her smell, her body, her hair, her flesh was always on me. I felt her pubes against my leg. She slept well, but I didn't. I never sleep well in a new environment. I looked at her in the night, pondered on her beauty, basked in the comfort of being with her.

In the morning, we sixty-nined, she on top of me; I licked her from cunt to asshole as she kept my cock deep into her mouth. She didn't come, but I did.

She had to get ready to go to class, and I had to go home. I had nothing to do there, though. I tried talking her into skipping class.

"Kiss me good-bye," she said.

I kissed her, gently, on the lips.

"That's no kiss," Mo said.

"You said you hated kissing."

"I say that to all strangers."

"I'm not a stranger?" I asked.

"After last night...?" she said.

We kissed for a good five minutes. Then I left.

HOLLOW HILLS

"This is the last night of my life," Cynthia says, "I mean, this is the last night of my life as a single woman, a single girl, this is the last night of that life and tomorrow I'll begin a new life so I want to do something I've never done before—well, I guess I am: I am doing something I've never done before. I'm here, aren't I? This is something I've never done before."

We're all crammed into Ralphie's 1971 Mustang. She's in back, wedged between Ajax, Mookie, and Fortanbras. They're passing around a bottle of Jim Beam. I'm up front, shotgun to Ralphie, who's driving.

"I hardly ever drink," Cynthia goes on, "but tonight I think I'll drink."

"Drink all you want," Mookie says.

Ralphie speeds up the speed, the Mustang's engine growls.

"I want to go somewhere I've never been before," Cynthia is saying, "somewhere strange, somewhere where you shouldn't go, somewhere with pizzazz and danger." She plays with her hair, that is pulled back into a bouncy-bouncy pony tail. "You know?" she says. I turn, take a quick glance at her, up and down. She wears a long, simple skirt; blue blouse; light green unbuttoned sweater. Her gold-rimmed glasses keep falling to the end of her nose. She doesn't wear any make-up.

"How about Hollow Hills?" Ajax says. "You ever been to Hollow Hills?" he asks Cynthia.

"No," she says. She was valedictorian in high school—"Miz Goody-Two-Shoes" in the locker room.

"Hollow Hills," Ajax says to Ralphie.

"Yeah," says Mookie.

Fortanbras nods, taking the bottle of Jim Beam from her.

Ralphie makes a turn.

I look at him.

He shrugs.

"Time to open some beer," Mookie says.

"Beer indeed," Fortanbras says.

"Shriek," Mookie says, "break out the brewskis!"

"I could go for a beer," Cynthia says.

I have the case of beer in my lap. I open it, pass beers out to all, except Ralphie. He doesn't drink and drive. I don't think I've ever seen him drink. I have a beer. I look in back. The guys seem to be squeezing Cynthia in more and more. Her glasses fall into her lap. "Oops," she says, picking them up, putting them on, drinking beer. "I'm getting buzzed," she announces.

"Only way to be," Ajax says.

"I feel good," she says.

"Only way to be," Ajax says.

There's an odd silence, the engine roars.

"Music," Cynthia says, "is there any music?"

"Thing with Ralphie," Mookie says, "is he don't like to hear tunes when he drives."

"Only the engine," Fortanbras says.

"Yeah," Ajax says.

Ralphie speeds up the speed.

"Where's these Hollow Hills?" she asks.

"We're getting there," Mookie says.

"Boy, are we," Fortanbras says.

"You two up there sure are quiet," Cynthia says to me and Ralphie.

"That's why they're up there," Ajax says.

"You should talk more," she says, directing this to Ralphie, "you should go blah-blah-blah."

I say, "Blah-blah-blah."

"You see?" she says. "You see how different things are when you go blah-blah-blah?"

Ralphie makes another quick turn.

"I spilled my beer," Fortanbras says.

"Here." I give him another.

I look back and see that Ajax is practically falling into Cynthia's lap. She's red in the face.

"It sure is getting cramped," she says

"That's what happens when you try to squeeze four people into the back," Mookie says.

"Someone's touching me," she says.

"That's me," Ajax says, "I have my hand caught under your ass."

"Stop that," she says.

"Are we there yet?" Mookie says.

"Not yet," Fortanbras says.

"Shriek," Cynthia says, "can I have another beer?"

I hand her one.

"You drank that other fast," Ajax says.

"I hardly ever get drunk," she says. "If I ever drink, it's one glass of wine, one can of beer, that's it. Tonight, I want to get smashed. I want to do something I've never done before. This is my last night, the last night I have to be a single person, and I want—I keep saying the same thing over and over, don't I?"

"Hey," Mookie says, "you can blah-blah-blah all you want."

"Yeah," Ajax says, "talk."

"Your hand is under my skirt," she says.

"It can't help itself."

"You're bad," she says.

"Um-hm," Ajax says.

"Stop that," she says again.

I see Ajax getting his hand higher in there and she doesn't protest.

Ralphie makes another quick turn and the four fall into each other more and more. Cynthia's head pokes up from a mass of bodies, arms, legs. "Help," she says, "help."

"Soon we'll be there," Mookie says, "then we can all get out."

"Maybe I should have sat up front," Cynthia says.

"Where would you sit?" Ajax asks.

"I could sit in Ralphie's lap," she says.

"He's driving."

"I could sit with Shriek," she says. "On his lap."

"That would keep it in the family," Fortanbras says.

"They're not family yet," Mookie says.

"Tomorrow," Cynthia says, "hey!"

"Hey, hey," Ajax says.

"Those are my panties," Cynthia says.

"Cotton," Ajax says, "I love cotton."

"I'm spilling my beer," she says.

"We all are," Mookie says.

Ralphie makes another sharp turn and the four in back make sounds like they're on a roller coaster. Wherever Cynthia is, back there, I can't see her. She's under the guys.

"Help," she says, muffled, "help."

"Oh," Fortanbras says, "everything is okay."

"Does he always drive like this?" she asks.

"Always," Ajax says.

"Get your hands out of my panties," she says, and her head emerges.

"It likes it there," Ajax says.

"My beer is all over the floor," she says.

"That's okay," Fortanbras says.

"You want another?" Mookie asks.

"Yes."

I give her one. Her arm struggles for it. Ajax's face is in her pony tail, Fortanbras' in her breasts.

"She's wet," Ajax says.

"She's hanging nip," Fortanbras says.

"Stop that," she says, "you're embarrassing me."

"That's why you have to drink a lot more," Mookie says, "so you won't be embarrassed."

Cynthia fights to get the can to her mouth and drink.

Ralphie takes another sharp turn.

"Where is he going?" Cynthia says.

"Hollow Hills," Fortanbras says.

"Is it this far?" she says.

"Not usually."

"Ouch," she says.

"Am I hurting you?" Ajax says.

"You really should stop that," she says.

"Just curious," he says, "we used to all call you Miz Goody-Two-Shoes, y'know."

"You did?"

"Yeah."

"Why?"

"You always had your nose in a book," Mookie says.

"So I like to read," she says, "what's wrong with that?"

"You never went out with anyone," Ajax says.

"I was shy," she says, "and your fingers are doing things they shouldn't."

"What's that you're doing, Ajax?" Fortanbras says.

"Trying to feel if what we expect is true," Ajax says. "I don't know, they're getting in there pretty easy."

"What is true?" Cynthia breaths.

"If you're a virgin."

"Why would you say that?"

"You never went out with anyone," Mookie says.

"Why would that make me a virgin?"

"Unless Shriek's brother got to you in secret," Fortanbras says. "Shriek, did your brother pop her?"

I shrug.

"You guys are too much," Cynthia giggles.

"She's very wet," Ajax says, "and she's no virgin."

"I'm done with this beer." She tosses the can to the floor.

Fortanbras is unbuttoning her blouse.

"When did you lose your cherry?" Ajax asks. "And who did it?"

"Now," she says, "that's none of your bees wax."

"I'm going to finger bang you," Ajax says, "I'm going to finger bang you until you come."

"Damn," Ralphie mutters, and makes a sharp turn, speeds up the speed, roars the engine.

The four in back all make more roller coaster sounds.

Someone's beer splashes onto the back of my head.

I say, "Hey, watch that."

"Sorry," says one of them.

I turn, see that Fortanbras is sucking on one of Cynthia's nipples, a pink nipple. Her sweater is pushed up, bra undone. Mookie has his pants down, is holding his penis.

"Take it," he says to Cynthia.

"Where's my glasses?" she says. "I lost my glasses."

"Take it," Mookie says.

"What? I can't see anything."

He grabs her hand, places it there.

"Oh," she says.

Ajax is doing something fierce with his hand under her skirt. "C'mon, Mis Goody-Two-Shoes," he says, "Miz Bookworm," he says, "come on my fist."

"You guys," she giggles, "you guys are just as crazy as when we were in high school."

"Jerk me off," Mookie says.

"Stop whining," she says, bending down and putting his penis in her mouth.

"Oh," Mookie says, "oh."

I look at Ralphie. He's concentrating on his driving.

The road is dark.

"Maybe here," I say.

He shakes his head.

"Or here," I say.

He shrugs, and turns, but not as sharply as before.

I look back. Mookie is making a strange face, his eyes closed. Cynthia's head bobs. "I'm coming," Mookie says, gasps, relaxes, and Cynthia's head stops.

She sits up, mouth wet. "Can I have another beer?"

"And open it for the lady this time," Fortanbras says, taking his mouth from her bosom.

I open a beer, give it to her.

"Thanks," she says, and drinks.

"I give up," Ajax says, taking his hand away.

"This beer is good," she sighs.

"We need to have some law and order back here," Ajax says.

Mookie moves to a corner so the others can straighten out.

"On my lap," Ajax says, "sit on my lap."

"Here," Ralphie mutters, and makes a sharp turn.

"Oh, oh, oh!" they all say in the back.

Cynthia is on Ajax's lap. His pants are down. She's facing me, with a smile, but I don't think she can see me. Her skirt is bunched up. Ajax enters her with his penis.

"Are we there yet?" she asks.

"Not yet," Ajax says.

"I'm going to come," she says, and screams.

"Finally," Ajax says, and comes.

She sits down between Ajax and Fortanbras.

"Beer?" she says.

I give her one.

"Thanks," she says, and drinks.

Fortanbras is stroking his penis.

She squints. "What are you doing?"

"Come on, Miz Goody-Two-Shoes. Suck this pecker-wood."

She bends down and takes him in her mouth.

I look at Ralphie.

He shrugs.

"Maybe here," I say.

He shakes his head.

"Maybe here?"

He shakes his head.

The road is dark.

I open a beer for myself.

I look in back. Fortanbras is shaking, eyes closed. Cynthia's head bobs. "Ahhhh," he says, grabbing at her pony tail. Her head stops. She sits up, spitting out thick white fluid. It dangles off her chin, swaying back and forth on a thin strand. "I still have beer," she says, drinking.

There's a long silence.

"This isn't the way," Ajax says.

Ralphie shrugs.

"My glasses!" Cynthia bends, picks up the gold-rims, puts them on. She smiles. "I can see now."

Ralphie takes a sharp turn.

Cynthia's legs are in the air.

The guys all start grabbing her.

"Stop that," she says, "you guys, you guys are something else!"

She sits up, adjusting her glasses. She pulls her skirt down, wipes her mouth on the sleeve of her sweater. "Is there any more beer?" she says.

"Should be plenty," Fortanbras says.

"Yes," I say.

Her hand is out.

I give her one.

"Oops," she says, seeing that her blouse is undone. She buttons it. She takes the beer from me. She drinks.

"She sure does drink," Mookie says, "for a bookworm."

"I'm going to have to pee soon," she says.

"You have to go?" Ajax says.

"Not yet," she says, "but I know I will soon."

"We'll all have to," Fortanbras says.

"'Cept Ralphie," Mookie says.

"Or Shriek," Ajax says. "Hey, Shriek, why aren't you drinking any?"

I hold up my beer. "I am."

"You should be back here," Mookie says.

"Maybe not," Ajax says, "it's a family thing."

"Not yet," Cynthia reminds him.

"Yeah," Ajax says, "tomorrow is the big day."

"Better hope Shriek doesn't tell his brother about all this," Fortanbras says.

"He won't," she says, looking at me, serious. "Will you?"

I don't say anything.

"And what could his brother say anyway?" She drinks. "I don't belong to him, yet. I have this final night. My one wild night. You don't think I don't know what happens at those bachelor parties? The strippers, the whatnot? The Going Out and Sowing Wild Oats? You don't think I know? I know. It's the way it is. Why can't it be the same for me? Why can't I sow my oats? Why can't I have a final night?"

"She has a point," Ajax says.

"I have to pee," she announces.

"She has to go," Mookie says.

"Ralphie!" Ajax says. "Think of the lady!"

Ralphie nods, stops the car. Ajax gets out, to let her out. She runs into a bush.

Ajax gets back in.

"Cold out there," he says.

"Dark," Mookie says.

"This is weird," Fortanbras says, "no one would believe us, no one."

"We're all here to back the story," Ajax says.

Mookie laughs. "We just did Miz Good Two-Shoes. What about Shriek and Ralphie? They gonna get some?"

"We're going to do her again," Ajax says, "we're going to take turns doing her all night long. Like she said, this is her last night."

"Choo-choo train," Mookie says.

"I'm lost," Ralphie says.

"What?" they say.

"I can't find Hollow Hills," he says.

"Shit," Ajax says, "are we lost?"

"I think I know the way back to town," I say.

"The hills," Mookie says, "we have to take her to the hills and do her there."

"Maybe we should just leave her here," Fortanbras says.

"What?" I say.

"This might be nothing but trouble," he says. "The girl's about to get married, we're looking for Hollow Hills and you know the curse those Injuns put there. Something bad is gonna to happen."

"Curse," Ajax laughs, "curse me arse!"

"We might meet some crazy psycho serial killer or something."

"Like Jason?" Mookie says. "Like Freddie?"

"I don't like this," Fortanbras says.

"She just sucked your dick," Ajax says, "and you say you don't like this?"

"Something doesn't feel right," Fortanbras says.

"We're lost," Ralphie says.

"We'll find our way back," I say.

Cynthia returns, sitting in the corner this time. There is a silence. "I feel better," she says.

Silence.

"Are we at Hollow Hills?" she asks.

"Not yet," Ajax says.

"We might be lost," Fortanbras says.

"Nah," Ajax says.

"We might be doomed," Fortanbras says.

"Oh," Ajax says, "shut up."

Cynthia adjusts her glasses.

I look at Ralphie. He speeds up the speed.

"Here," I say softly, pointing, "this is the way back to town."

He takes the sharp turn.

Ajax, Mookie, and Fortanbras all fall into Cynthia, but they move away and give her space.

"I really had to pee," she says, adjusting her glasses, checking her blouse.

I turn around. "Want another beer?"

She shakes her head. "No, I've had enough."

SANDRA BOISE TURNS THIRTY

A.

Ah, my friend Sandra Boise's birthday is tomorrow. She is turning thirty and not happy about it.

"My thirtieth was great," I tell her while we are at the bar and getting drunk. "I was living with this woman, Terrah, and dating another woman, a married woman, her name was Irene."

"Wait," says Sandra, "you were seeing a married woman?"

"It was cool."

"Maybe for the two of you, but what about her husband and your girlfriend?"

"Her husband didn't know, and Terrah and I had an understanding."

"Oh, an 'understanding.' Uh-huh."

Now I get annoyed: "Would you *let* me tell my story?"

She rolls her eyes. "Tell."

"Terrah was bi, so I could fool around with other women as long as she could have sex with them too," I say. I'm sure my voice sounds nostalgic with the fine memories of sexual encounters from the past. "Irene didn't care for having lesbian experiences, so she had no interest in Terrah. This was bugging Terrah; she felt like I was having an affair. She felt left out. I told Irene this. Terrah threw me a huge birthday bash when I turned thirty. Irene wanted to make it special. At the party she said she was ready. 'Ready for what?' I said. She said she was ready to have sex with Terrah; she would do this as a birthday present. I was like, 'Yeah!'"

"I bet you were."

"I thought it was the best birthday present ever."

"You were *excited*."

"I got hard just listening to her words. Irene wanted to get naked right there in the middle of the party. We just needed to find Terrah. We found her in the bedroom. Perfect place, right? But she was drunk."

"Like us?"

"We're not drunk yet."

"Getting there," Sandra says, and waves at the bartender for another round.

"The problem with Terrah," I tell her, "she was passed out."

"She was that drunk."

"Yeah. We tried to wake her up"

"To have sex?"

"That's what we were there for. Listen, Boise, are you going to let me tell my story or not?"

"Am I interrupting?"

"Aren't you always?"

"So I'll keep my mouth shut," she says. "Where were you? Oh yeah, you and Irene were gonna fuck Terrah but Terrah was passed out."

"Needless to say," I say, "I was greatly disappointed. But Irene was getting undressed. So I pulled off all of Terrah's clothes."

Sandra is about to say something but stops herself.

"Yes," I say, "Terrah was asleep but I wanted her naked. Just in case she woke up. So Irene and I get on the bed and we have sex next to Terrah's body. Then we have sex on her body. It was hot. I came on Terrah's skin and

Irene and I rubbed it all over her. That was my thirtieth birthday."

B.

Booze. After a couple more drinks, Sandra Boise says, "I have a kinky birthday tale. Let me tell it and you better not interrupt me, motherfucker, because you know how I like my running, rambling monologues, and this is one: I'm twenty-one, I'm twenty and about to turn twenty-one, and I've been dating this guy, this older guy (by older I mean he's like twenty-five; okay, I'm lying, he's thirty-five, okay?) and so he says to me: 'So what do you want for b-day twenty-one? Go out to a bar and get shit-faced drunk?' and I say: 'No, what I would like for my birthday is to fuck you in the ass with a strap-on.' He takes a pregnant pause (I like that phrase) and he goes: 'Are you serious?' I tell him of course I'm serious and he says why and I tell him because ever since I was a bat out of high school I've had fantasies of fucking men with strap-ons. 'Look,' I say, 'you like me to lick your asshole, so I bet you'd like me to fuck your asshole.' 'Look,' he says, 'I fuck you there, you don't fuck me there.' 'Look,' I say, 'this is my birthday wish, okay?' 'Okay,' he says…. Later…after I lick his asshole real good, after I get my nose and tongue up there, he says, 'You can have your birthday present.' So next week my birthday arrives and I have bought this especially big strap-on dildo to fuck him with and I didn't expect him to like it. You want to know the truth? I wanted to hurt him. I wanted to hurt him because I didn't really like him, he was too old for me, and I thought maybe this would be a good way to get rid of him. I'd have some fun, he'd be ashamed, or angry, and that would be that. But no, that is not what happened. You wanna know what happened? The guy loved it. He screamed with joy. He said I opened him up to new possibilities, he said I made his soul soar, he said I showed him his true self with that fake dick up his ass and he wanted me to fuck him all the time. All the time. So I did. And I got bored with it. So I dumped him. He was very depressed."

C.

Cab. We're taking a taxi, Sandra Boise and I, because we're now too damn drunk to drive. We leave the bar. We take a cab. I guess we're going back to her place. In the cab, she reaches over and grabs my crotch. She says, "Yum. Yum. And yum?"

"What?"

"I'm *in the mood.*"

"How rare."

"We're just friends," she says, moving her hand away.

I grab her hand and put it back.

"Oh?" she says.

"Friendly friends," I say.

That old Bauhaus song runs through my mind, "A Spy in the Cab."

D.

"Dick, I love dick," says Sandra Boise, and gives me a blow job the first thing after we step inside her studio apartment. It's a cramped place and she has a Murphy bed.

E.

"Eat my pussy," she says fifteen minutes later, naked on her Murphy bed, pushing my head into her crotch, "eat that kitty and eat it long and good, fucker...."

F.

"Feet," she sighs an hour later. "Lick my feet, suck my toes," and she puts her right foot up to my mouth. "You into feet fetish stuff?"

"No."

"You are now."

"Yes," I say, and put her big toe in my mouth.

G.

"Get on your knees," I tell her.

Sandra Boise is in the bathtub. I hold my placid cock. She closes her eyes. I start to pee on her.

H.

"Happy birthday," I tell her as we take a shower together, getting sober.

"I'm not thirty yet," she says softly. "Tomorrow, yes. But not today."

I.

"I want a special birthday present from you," says Sandra Boise after the shower. We dry each other off with one dirty towel.

"To fuck me in the ass with a strap-on?" I say. "Sure, you can do that. I can get into that."

"I have a different unfulfilled fantasy," she says.

"Yeah?"

"Yeah. I want to menstruate on a man."

"What?"

"Call it a bloody shower. Not golden, not brown, but red."

"You've done this before?"

"No. No, you idiot, that's why I want it for a birthday present. I've been thinking about it for years. No guy I've dated would do it. I can't even get guys to fuck me when I'm on my period."

"Why not? Warm and squishy."

"See, I knew you'd be into it. Because you're a pervert."

J.

I jack off on her birthday, while on my back, legs up, as Sandra Boise fucks me with her strap-on dick. I like it but she's bored. She's thirty now.

K.

"Okay," Sandra Boise says, "I'm ready now."

It's a week later. I'm lying naked on her bathroom floor. She's naked and squatting over me. She's on her period. Her flow flows slowly like a lost dream onto my skin. She moves up and down my body, the blood like a line of ink. She moves her pussy over my face. I taste her and she tastes like something from my distant childhood that I can't determine.

She looks down at me, at the blood. She rubs it into my skin, like I rubbed my semen into Terrah's flesh that birthday night long ago.

"Why?" I ask.

"Because it's so dirty," she says.

L.

"I love you," she says before I leave. "Now."

MOVEMENTS

I. SUITE FOR AN END TO A MARRIAGE

The first time I saw my wife fucking another man, she was by our Jacuzzi the night of The Party. I was fairly convinced it would be the last party we'd throw as husband and wife.

Actually, she was with two men. One was a fellow I didn't know and he was fucking her from behind his large, hairy hands tightly grasping her hips in an attempt to control the backward thrust of her pelvis as if she were a wild animal. The other one (my best friend) had his dick in her mouth. She was taking this dick down her throat pretty deep, and he was no bigger than myself. She never did that for me. Maybe she never liked my dick; and this is something I could believe, given the recent sour circumstances of our marriage.

"I don't think I'm in love with you anymore," she told me three months ago. I was trying to have sex with her. Her pussy was dry like a dry cunt. Finally she pushed my hand away and said she didn't want to. We hadn't made love in quite a while.

"What do you mean?"

"Is it hard to understand?" she said. "How can I illustrate it any better? *I don't think I'm in love with you anymore.*"

"I see," I said.

"No," she said, "you don't."

We tried the marriage counselor routine, and that only proved to drive us further apart, snickering at all the flowery, New Age suggestions the counselor was trying to sell us.

"What a fucking waste of money," my wife said.

Her name is Beryl, by the way.

* * * * * * *

I stood there, looking out the kitchen window, and watched Beryl fuck. The one who was my best friend, his name is Art.

I wasn't surprised. The night seemed to be heading for this. Beryl was on the war path to have sex with someone other than me.

"I'm feeling frisky tonight," she said when she pulled me aside during The Party.

She was drunk. I told her so.

"So I'm *drunk*," she said, "and I'm feeling *good*."

I wasn't feeling good. "Thanks for the information."

"I just want you to know," she said, "that I might do something *wild*, I might do something *sexy*, and I don't want you to get in the *way*."

"I won't," I said.

"I don't want you to get in the way of my being *happy*."

"I won't," I said.

It started, I suppose, with her dance or striptease. She put on some electronic music, the kind that gives me a headache. I don't know where she got this music. She began to dance, and had an audience of men, cheering as she lifted her skirt and flashed her panties; and when she opened her blouse, and exposed her tits. She had small, pointed, brown breasts. She was a tall, slender woman with long legs and tanned skin and straight blonde hair, a very appealing woman to many men.

"That's some wife of yours!" someone said to me, slapping me on the back.

"Yeah," I said.

Beryl had stripped down to her thongs. Drunken hands groped for her. One pair of hands belonged to Art. Beryl giggled, and ran out back, and jumped into the Jacuzzi.

Watching her fuck, I knew it was the hottest sight I'd ever viewed. It was better than watching a porno: this was real.

I wasn't the only person watching, either. Several men, some I knew, some I didn't, moved toward the threesome. I moved with them. We were all like mesmerized cattle.

* * * * * * *

Two months ago, I was sitting in a bar with Art. We were on our fourth or fifth drinks.

"I think Beryl and I are getting a divorce," I said.

"You think?" Art said.

"Probably," I said. "She doesn't love me anymore."

"No."

"Yes."

"No."

"She said this."

"Do you still love her?" he asked.

"I'm not sure," I said. "I think I do."

"What went wrong? You two used to be the happy fun couple."

"I'm not sure," I said. "I think she might be having an affair."

"You *think*?"

"I wouldn't put it past her."

HOW TO HAVE AN AFFAIR, BY HEMMINGSON

* * * * * * *

When Beryl was done with Art and the man I didn't know, she started having sex with two other men. The Party was becoming something else. Other people departed old friends, giving me strange looks. Someone said, "You didn't say this was going to turn into an *orgy*." It was past one in the morning anyway, the time for most parties to start winding down.

Art, with his clothes back on, passed me.

I grabbed his arm.

"Hey," he said softly.

I just looked at him.

"We should talk," he said.

"Yeah," I said.

* * * * * * *

The Party was over, people were gone. Four A.M., I lay in bed, listening to my wife taking a bath. The door was unlocked. I went in. She stared at me. She was sitting in the tub, water and soap all around her. She started to say something, I held up a finger to stop her. I unzipped my pants and showed her my hard prick.

"Do you plan to do something with that?" she said.

"I have some ideas," I said.

"You look all worked up."

"I am that," I said.

"I haven't seen your dick that bulging and red since... since we first met."

I approached her, my body shaking. "Did you like fucking those men tonight?"

Softly: "You know I did."

"I could tell. I haven't seen you fuck like that since... since we first met."

She said: "Did you like me fucking those men?"

94

I grabbed Beryl's head. I was fast and she was surprised. I pushed her face into my crotch. I bunched up her slick wet hair in my fists, like I was angry. I was more horny than angry, or a fine line that crosses both conditions. She took my cock in her mouth. I wondered how many loads of come she swallowed this evening. Mine would be just another. Beryl pulled my pants down, grabbed at the flesh of my ass, yanking me forward, so that I was partially in the water with her, getting wet....

* * * * * * *

In bed, I asked her how long she'd been fucking Art. I knew that tonight wasn't the first time the way they were with each other: that familiarity of the body. Beryl said, "For a while now."

II. SONATA FOR A NEW PHASE IN MARRIAGE

The three of us were in the Jacuzzi. This was inevitable, this had to happen; I knew it, Beryl knew it, Art knew it.

We'd had dinner. It was a quiet dinner. I savored every bite of the mushroom sautéed chicken Beryl had prepared, the scalloped potatoes that reminded me of being a child and eating mother's well-cooked meals. It was a warm night. Beryl suggested we relax in the Jacuzzi, drink wine. Art wanted beer. Beryl drank wine. We got naked, acting like excited, modest teenagers doing something daring and naughty, and went into the water.

It was a clear night out, a lot of stars.

I was also drinking wine.

"That's Mars up there." Beryl pointed at the sky, to a bright star with a red tint.

"Think there's life up there?" Art said.

"Mars? Or elsewhere?"

"Mars."

"Sure," she said.

"What do you think?" Art asked me.

"As long as they don't invade us," I said, "I don't care."

"I'm glad you're not mad," he said.

"I'm not mad," I said. "I keep telling myself I should be. But I'm not."

"It's good that you're not," Beryl said. "It means you're growing. It means you're moving in the direction I am, and that makes me happy."

Art waded through the water, to her direction. She giggled. He backed her against the Jacuzzi wall. They kissed. I sipped my glass of wine and watched him kiss her. I watched him lift her body up, sit her on the edge of the Jacuzzi, spread her legs, and go down on her. Beryl liked this. She ran her fingers through his wet hair and made familiar sounds of pleasure. I knew those sounds like a distant cousin one has fond memories of. She leaned back, propping herself on her elbows, letting Art work his tongue between her legs, his hairy hands rubbing her stomach and breasts. She looked at me and said, "Come here and stick that dick in my mouth."

I got out of the water. The hair on my body was matted, I was dripping. I liked walking about like this, my cock pointing the way. I crouched before Beryl so she could take me in her mouth as Art continued to eat her pussy, grunting sounds coming from his throat.

We then moved away from the Jacuzzi, to a lounge chair, where she sucked on us both: Art and I standing close, almost touching skin, Beryl going from one cock to another. I could smell Art's body. I could smell the musk from his crotch, and I wondered if I was emitting any odors he could sense. Needless the say, the smell of sex permeated the immediate air around us.

We took turns fucking my wife. Art went first. I wanted to watch them; watching them made me want her all the more.

"Whore," I whispered in her ear when it was my turn.

"Yeah," she said, "talk dirty to me."

When we went to the bed, Beryl wanted us both inside her at the same time. "One in my kitty," she said with a seductive voice, touching herself, "and one in my booty."

* * * * * * *

"I have hope for us," she said later.

We were lying in bed, alone. The sex had been good. I remembered a night, not a month ago, when we were in bed together, and she said, "We should just have wild sex right now, that'd solve all our problems," but neither of us could do it.

"That's good," I said.

"I really do." She kissed me.

I kissed her back.

"I feel so sexual, so alive again. I want to fuck more men. I want to fuck *a lot* of men. I love you. Will you help me do this?"

* * * * * * *

She could have done it by herself, or with Art, but she wanted me involved, and I wanted to be involved. And Art, of course, wished to be there too.

It started with the gangbang. Art made the arrangements for this, being the resourceful fellow that he is, getting the guys Beryl had fucked at The Party together for another go at it. There were nine of them in all, more than I had originally imagined. Had my wife really fucked nine men that night? I suppose so. Ten, including Art. Eleven, including myself.

If I ever thought that what happened was just a wild fantasy, or a dream, I have the evidence on videotape. It was, yes, Art's idea to capture this night for posterity. When he suggested it to Beryl, she got this wild look in her eyes and said, "Yes." I was beginning to know that look better and better. I wanted her to say no. I wanted her to say no because I liked the idea myself.

(A number of times, alone, feeling lonely, thinking of the life I once had, I will put that tape into the VCR, and watch. I will watch my wife fuck all those men in a single session, fucking her in every combination possible.

Others have watched her. Hundreds, thousands, all over the world. This is really what this story is about.)

* * * * * * *

It was Art's idea again to create a web site and place stills from the gang-bang video on it. He created the web page, and allowed people to access it for free. In a matter of days, the site was getting thousands of hits. Art said this was a combination of posting stills to various news groups with sexual themes, and the help of a number of search engines.

After a month, he or we announced that the whole video tape could be purchased for $34.95.

In a matter of weeks, 2,000 orders came in.

First we were just some people doing kinky things, and now we were in business.

We were, I guess you can say, pornographers.

* * * * * * *

IV. SOLO IN THE JACUZZI, WITH MEMORY

I was alone in the Jacuzzi. It was another clear night. That red star was indeed Mars. I stared at it. I wanted to go there. I wondered what sex life was like on Mars.

In the bedroom, in the house, Art and Beryl were fucking. He was fucking her in the ass when I had left, and came out here, turned on the jet streams, and sat in the warm bubbling water. And closed my eyes while looking up.

In the water, I thought about the two of them. I pictured his cock going in and out of her butt, the muscles of her sphincter contracting with each thrust. The more I thought of this, I started to become aroused. The image in my head was far more enticing than returning to the bedroom and seeing and smelling it. In my mind, I was the director, I was in control, and I made my own movie of the act.

I also pictured scenes from the night of The Party.

I touched myself. I had my cock in my hand, under the water, and I began to jack-off.

I watched my semen clump in the water, floating to the top, getting caught in a whirlwind of bubbles, spinning around, blending in with water and chlorine.

INTERMISSION: How We Met

I met Beryl at the recital of an experimental cellist; he was on tour for his new CD. In the first half of his performance, he presented classical pieces by Debussy and Mozart. I had difficulty listening. I kept glancing at the blonde woman who was sitting alone, across from me in the small concert hall. She was wearing black slacks and a white cotton blouse. She kept looking at me as well. We talked during the intermission. Small talk: what do you think of the cellist? Oh, he's good. We sat together for the second half, and the cellist presented his own iconoclastic work, hooking his instrument to microphones, adding special effects, or playing along with a tape full of strange sounds. Towards the end, he did a manic solo and broke two strings. After, I asked the blonde woman Beryl if she'd like to go get some coffee. "No," she said, "but how about a beer?" Two months later, we were living together. Six months later, we were married.

V. QUARTET

"We've been approached with a business deal," Art said on the phone. Beryl and I were both on separate phones in the house, different rooms, listening.

"Go on," she said.

He said, "There's this couple here in the city who have a successful on-line business. They do the same as us: sell videos and pix of them fucking, or the wife fucking some guys. Then they started to make and distribute vids of other couples. Acting as distributors, growing their business. You know. They came across our web site, and they want Beryl. I mean, they can sell five times the amount of videos we do. So they say."

"What does this mean?" I said.

"More money," Art said.

"More money," Beryl said, "sounds good to me."

* * * * * * *

This couple Fred and Donna invited the three of us to dinner, to talk about the possibility of a business venture. Art drove in his own car, and was late. Beryl and I were both nervous and we didn't know why.

They had a nice, modesty furnished suburban house, not the kind of place you'd think a big Internet porn outfit would be located. Fred and Donna were also the kind of couple you might see at a PTA meeting modestly and almost conservatively dressed, quiet, and friendly. They were in their late thirties, attractive, and unassuming.

Over dinner, we talked about our lives, not sex.

I wondered why I was here. I was expecting drugs, hard booze, triple-X love acts.

Fred suggested we go to the water.

They also had a Jacuzzi, but this one could fit ten people. It was very nice and spacious. Fred and Donna disrobed before us, and got in. Donna was a bit on the chubby side, but had a magnificent tan and silicone-enhanced breasts. Fred, I was quick to notice, didn't have a hair on his well-muscled body, and a dick that had to be ten inches long.

Art stripped and jumped in. Beryl and I took our clothes off, slowly, still uncertain, and joined the party.

We were all drinking champagne, by the way. It always begins with some kind of party.

"You have a great body," Donna said to Beryl.

"Thank you," Beryl said.

"I'd love to fuck you," Donna said.

"I'm not bi," Beryl said.

"Too bad," Donna said. "But maybe Fred can fuck you. I like to watch him fuck other women."

"Sounds good to me," Beryl laughed.

"You got a look-see at his tool?" Donna said.

"Oh yes," Beryl said. "I wonder if I could take it."

"It takes some getting used to," Donna said. "His cock is very nice."

"Yeah," Beryl said.

Art and I looked at each other.

"Let's talk business," Fred said.

"Let's," Art said.

"This past year," Fred said, "we've cleared three million in sales."

I almost choked on my champagne. Beryl did.

"You're shitting me," Art said.

"No," Fred said.

Donna smiled. "We'll make more each year."

"Porn is the backbone of e-commerce," Fred said, "and the amateur market is in a boom. A huge boom. There are dozens, hundreds of people like us making a living off pleasure. We have something many people out there want."

"Intimacy," Donna said, "and love."

"This business saved our marriage," Fred said. He drew Donna close to him. They held each other. They kissed. "We wouldn't be together now," he went on. "It added...excitement. It delivered us from an absolutely droll life, the same thing day after day. You know what I mean."

"I was ready to leave him," Donna said. "I wanted something more."

"We both did," Fred said.

"And we found it," Donna said.

Beryl and I looked each other. I moved to kiss her. She kissed me. Art looked away.

"We like what you have," Donna said.

"We can get rich together," Fred said.

"I like the sound of that," Beryl said.

"Me too," I said.

Fred said, "So let's fuck and seal the deal."

We all laughed.

"Hey, buddy," Fred said to Art, "there's a camera in the house, and a light. Why don't you get it?"

Art nodded, and got out of the water. He looked lonely, walking away wet and naked. I can't say that I felt sorry for him.

Donna moved to me, and Beryl moved to Fred. I took Donna's large breasts in my hands and rubbed them. Her pink nipples were pointing at me. Beryl was stroking

Fred's big dick and she said something like, "Oh my." He sat on the edge of the spa, and Beryl did her best to take him in her mouth.

"You want me to suck your dick too?" Donna whispered. "What do you want me to do? I'll do anything, anything."

Art set up the camera.

Donna and I got out of the water to fuck. I had her on her back, her thick legs on my shoulders. She smelled strong of perfume. She reached up and bit my nipple as I fucked her. Beryl was still sucking on Fred.

"Hey," Fred said, turning to me with a smile. "I think I'm about to come in your wife's mouth."

Art didn't join us. As he operated the video camera, he jerked-off. He was now an observer. I could see it on his face: something was missing. He looked lonely and I didn't care.

VI. EPILOGUE

Our hair was still wet when we got in the car. We were electrified. The sex had been good, the idea of success even better.

I touched my wife's face.

"We don't need Art," she said.

"I was thinking the same thing."

"Our marriage will work, won't it?"

"I hope so."

"We can be as happy and wealthy as Donna and Fred."

I wanted to say that we *were* Donna and Fred. We'd just made love to our mirror images, and it was caught on tape.

I started the car.

"Turn on the heater," Beryl said. "I don't want to catch cold."

I did, and as we drove, the warmth started at our feet, and moved up our bodies and to our faces. We were holding hands the whole way.

Home, our hair dry, we went into our own Jacuzzi and fucked in the water and under the stars, and there was only us, and it was very nice again, for awhile.

MOMENTS

Everything is relative in the middle of September—for instance, a hotel room in Sebha at four in the morning, after driving from Tripoli. It was the last time Dominique and I had fucked; or the last time I remembered fucking her. I'm not exactly certain.

I had walked around for two hours waiting for her to wake up after the drive.

It was still summer and an unbearable heat radiated everywhere. I wandered the sparsely populated market area, bought a carton of Camels out of the back of a giant, dilapidated truck with Niger plates—smuggled all the way from the coast, I thought.

This had always been a crossroads for everything illegal: drugs, booze, people.

When I returned to our room, Dominique was coming around; no air-con, sweat all over the bed and clothes sticking to her in the wrong places. She was small and dark, brown eyes and hair, a big smile with a lot of white teeth. She had been in some real shitholes: smuggling drugs to the Zapatistas; working with some kind of cultural group in Vietnam back in '96; sharing a squat in Istanbul with hashish-smoking human rights investigators. She was wicked smart and had a temper. I'd met her my first year of college and I had no idea what she was doing here, with me, at the emptiest end of the Sahara.

—Where you been?

—Around, I said, there's not a lot to see here; we can rest for a day or two, maybe check out that noise the car's making.

The car, a Range Rover of unknown vintage, was falling apart. I had my doubts it would cough along much longer.

I sat down next to her on the narrow bed. She leaned against me and made a face, and I could feel the heat on her skin. Her body stank and I was used to it, as I'm sure she was used to my human stench by now. This is what happens over time, the heat, the desert. I touched her hair and ribbed her neck. We were quiet, and the world was quiet outside; we touched each other and said nothing. She leaned back and began pulling off her shirt; it came off sticky, with a fight. Her small breasts were bare; no bras here in Africa; dark nipples stiffening in the cool pre-dawn breeze that began blowing through the open window like a childhood memory.

I leaned down and began sucking on her little tits.

She was trying to help me pull off my pants, getting everything more tangled. I stood up and slid them off. She was naked and watching me. The bed was covered in deep shadows; I couldn't see her face well and I didn't need to. I didn't want to.

I lay down on top of her, my hand down between her legs. She was real hairy, an unshaven bush that felt abnormal. I could feel—*and hear*—her getting wetter; her pubes slick like a morning slime.

—I don't have a condom, I said.

—I don't care, she said.

She arched her hips, wrapped her legs around my waist. I started to fuck her, and the more we fucked the more wildcat it got. She started to thrash on the bed and make little crying noises so I had to heavily lay on top of her, press her into the bed, stifle her. Didn't want the sex police kicking in the door. I was starting to see that spinning dizziness that meant I was going to come soon. When I did, I thrust once or twice, and fell back. She rolled away, back into the sheets.

* * * * * * *

We stayed in town for two days, enough time to buy groceries, fix the arthritic car and make sure the road ahead was clear of drifting sand, landmines, intermittent fighting, all that fun North African stuff. We set out early in the morning for Ghat, the border crossing with Algeria. I wanted to go further south, cross at Tumu, but Dominique had insisted. Wanted to use her French, I guess. I don't like to have serious talks while driving. Casual conversation, that's okay. But these involved, emotional discussions about relationships and sex, lying and betrayal— I'd rather go to some foul-smelling coffee shop and drink mud. It fucks the road up, you miss the curves, don't get the jumps off the line....

The last year, we were living together and it was either she jumping me after she'd drink too much, or I paying her. I was jerking off four or five times a day because she hadn't been that interested in sex. She had been living in France for the last few months, doing her junior year abroad. I'd had some encounters, but on our small campus, if I fucked anyone, it would be hard to keep it from the general public.

I did get a blowjob from a freshman named Rita: long dreadlocks and big tits. She'd sucked me off in the laundry room of my apartment complex and the noise her mouth made competed with the tumbling dryers. She seemed all right, we went for drinks a few times, but then she ran off with the assistant registrar and I never saw her again.

Like Kurt Vonnegut once wrote generations ago: *So it goes.*

HOW TO HAVE AN AFFAIR, BY HEMMINGSON

* * * * * * *

I met up with Dominique in Paris; we rented the car, drove down through Italy, caught the ferry to Malta, spent a week in the mild sun and surf, then took the one ferry to Tripoli. We headed for the Atlantic coast of West Africa, somewhere around Lagos. The heat and emptiness recharged our sex; we'd fucked more in the last twelve days than we had in the last twelve months.

We ran into trouble at the Ghat crossing. The oldest story: our papers weren't in order. While I was trying to straighten it out with my bad Arabic, Dominique was talking to three of the border guards. She was actually flirting with them—touching her hair, laughing and bending forward to show a little tit. They kept pressing in closer and closer to her; I could see their hands patting her shoulder; they were complimenting her hair.

The implied danger aroused me. I tried to keep my mind on dealing with the customs guy, but all I could picture was watching Dominique get dragged behind the guard shack by these three and getting brutally and royally fucked—one in her mouth and the other taking her from behind on the barren sand while the third jerks off in her hair. Their fucking would be the only sounds for miles; she'd gag and take all of the semen that would pour into her mouth. I was getting hard thinking about it, my dick throbbing in time with the sound of idling car engines.

We finally got everything settled and we were able to drive on.

A few days later the car died, one hundred miles from the coast. We walked for hours, fighting about whose fault it was. When we reached the next village, we were through. She caught the first bus south, and that was that, I never saw her again....

I think.

I'm not sure.

HOW TO HAVE AN AFFAIR, BY HEMMINGSON

It's all a blur now, like our entire relationship….

* * * * * * *

Honestly, I can't remember anymore. Maybe it was some new type of hell that I've decided didn't happen. She still lives over there, in Europe. HOTEL TERMINUS, the Klaus Barbie place. Lyon. A mutual friend told me she was marrying some eighteen-year-old German kid with a nine inch-cock.

The strangest thing about the trip is that I never knew where we were. I fixate on *place*; I must know where I am when traveling, a mental reference, a name to access certain files of gray matter. I cannot locate it on any map. No idea where the house was in Marseilles, back when she was going to school; the chapel along the cliffs where we all almost fell off because of the wind. The bar by the docks in Valletta, a 250-pound dog lying in the narrow entrance, too long to step over. I am cartographically fixated.

What I even remember of that whole blurry period is off. Dominique had been late picking me up at the airport; turns out she had gotten drunk with some Belgians and passed out in a bathtub. She showed up after an hour. I was in the airport bar drinking with someone I think was named "Marie." Dominique dragged me off and into the Metro, and took me to a hotel room she's rented so we could spend a night away from her smelly French roommates.

I hadn't gotten laid in months; I don't know about her.

We checked in, walked up to the room, and attacked each other. Seriously, we ripped each other's clothes off, threw each other around the room like POWs being interrogated. She attacked my balls with relish, squeezing so hard I thought they're going pop like small balloons in the sadistic hands of a little bully.

Before I knew it I was coming in her mouth; then we switched and I was going down on her, flicking her clit with my tongue, sucking on it hard, she was screaming, bucking, slapping me on the head and telling me to eat her foreign filth.

We fucked twice, nothing special, a few positions, nothing too freaky, we were just getting used to each other's movements again, each other's taste and smell and souls....

* * * * * * *

Later that night, I was drinking a bottle of Red Label with a stranger who was one of her friends; he was manic and frightened me. He was bi, kept rubbing my thigh, asking if he could call me *Charlie*. (I found out later this was the name of one of his male cousins that he'd fucked up the asshole.) I said was flattered, but not really into it tonight.

The last day Dominique and I were in France, before we left for Africa, I was out with Monsieur Bisexual—his name was Jean. We were having beers with people in a weird and fucked-up neighborhood on the north side of Paris: lots of crumbly buildings, it had just rained and everything smelled like rats and shit and rat shit. We'd been at it for a while, really tearing into the liquor, sometimes going into the bathroom and smoking hash; everyone was pretty gone, and after a lot of hours went by, the group decided to go home.

Jean pulled me aside.

—Take a walk with me, he said.

He was huge, six-three easy, maybe 230 pounds. I think he was from the far western part of France, Brittany. Dark all over, like an Arab.

—I don't know, Jean, I told him, we're pretty pixilated; maybe we should go back with everyone else.

—Nothing funny; I want to show you something.

I was feeling displaced. We walked for a while, not saying much. It was late and there aren't a lot of people out.

—I'm sorry about that first night you were here, all that sloppy shit I laid on you, he said.

—Forget about it.

—Do you want another drink?

—Sure.

We went into a small bar and sat along the back wall, drinking Kronenbourg draft. Jean was telling me about his childhood on the coast, his three years in the army. I noticed a woman looking at us from the bar. She was thin and pale, long blonde hair. I noticed a tattoo of a purple koi peeking out from the small of her back. She was wearing jeans and a white tank top. Armpit hair, of course, wispy blonde.

She smiled, looked away, looked back.

Jean followed my stare.

—You like her?

—Yeah, I said.

Jean was up and moving. He sat next to her, said something quietly. She leaned back and looked at me again; nodded and said something to Jean.

They got up and left.

—What the fucking fuck, I said to no one in particular.

Jean stuck his head back in through the front door of the bar.

—Are you coming or not?

I tossed a few euros on the bar and walked out. They were about ten feet ahead of me, walking side by side down the street. Their hands were resting on each other's asses. I could see Jean's hand squeeze her, pinch her flesh. She jumped, laughed, hit his arm. They sidelines into an alley that ran along a huge building that looked like a hospital.

The woman led Jean down a staircase and onto a small landing. She quickly stripped out of her jeans and tank top. Jean pulled his pants off. She was on her knees, working his balls with her right hand while licking up and down the length of his dick. I have to admit: he had a beautiful cock, long and curved, pretty fat, nice color.

I was impressed, not jealous.

I wasn't sure what I was supposed to be doing. My hand went down into my own pants. She was working her left hand around to Jean's asshole, I could see the fingers slide into his crack, and when I saw his body stiffen I knew she was probing that pucker. Jean looked over at me, semi-glassy eyed.

—Take them off, he said.

I unbuckled, slid my pants down around my boots and kind of walk-shuffled over to them. The woman let go of Jean's balls and grabbed mine. She popped his cock all the way into her mouth and really jammed two of her fingers into his ass. Jean was pumping, fucking this woman's mouth, moving between her fingers and mouth like he was an engine. When he came, I thought I could hear it splash against her throat. She pulled back and started in on my cock without a word. I really want to fuck her; she was too quick for me. Jean's semen was dripping off her lips and was hot and coated my own dick. I came almost immediately; Jean watched closely and rubbed my neck as this anonymous girl drank everything I gave her, slurping noisily while her fingers started play with my asshole.

I sat down on a garbage can and tried to recover my wits as she wiped her lips and face with a handkerchief. Jean pulled out a wad of bills from his pocket, counts off a few, gave them to her. She kissed us both on the cheek, smelling like stale sperm, and then walked away.

Jean and I sat there.

—I won't say anything to Dominique, he said.

—There's really no reason not to.

—I think she would be more upset by my being here than by you getting sucked off by a common *sale putain*, he said.

—Yeah? I said.

—She is tired of me seeing her friend's cocks, he said with a shrug.

—I'm sure, I said.

He laughed and then I laughed too.

—That's her, I said.

—That *is* our Dominique, he said.

We had a moment, laughing and patting each other on the back, and then we stood up and left the alley.

THE BRILLIANCE AND MISERY OF
BODIES; OF WAR, OF DREAMS

Like many idealistic young Ivy League men in 1917, he signed up as a volunteer ambulance driver for the Red Cross. His name was Roland. He was going to Europe, and Elizabeth didn't want him to go. She was also a student of the Ivy League crust, and she was in love with Roland; they'd already made plans to get married. Roland was set on this decision to go this was to be a great adventure, after all, and many young men of his acquaintance were also doing the same.

I can finish school when I return, he told Elizabeth, and I'll come back much more prepared for life—*our* life.

And he kissed her.

Elizabeth decided she would give herself to him before he left; and in the back of Roland's Model T, he made her a woman. It was painful and uncomfortable and Elizabeth didn't like it at all. She held onto Roland after, and cried.

Did I hurt you? he asked.

I'm afraid I'll never see you again, she said.

Of course you'll see me again, he said.

He didn't come back from Europe. He was unaccounted for; he was presumed dead. Elizabeth knew he was dead she'd known this would happen the night in his car. She kept dreaming of all sorts of horrid scenarios, until the real news arrived.

That's when she began drinking.

She made a point to attend as many parties she could, where she could drink, laugh, dance, forget; and find men to have sex with.

Sex was no longer uncomfortable, but an evasion. She could close her eyes, her body tumult with alcohol and cocaine; it was nice to get lost into the sensation of a man's cock moving in and out of her. She never imagined these men to be Roland (she couldn't do that to herself). They were just men, and she knew it was her lot, maybe mission, to have sex with any man who wanted her; in the name of Roland, and all he missed in this life. She didn't care. She was taking something from them, little pieces that were slowly filling her. She was taking, and they didn't know—they thought *they* were the ones taking, and this perverse knowledge of her secret mission gave her great pleasure.

She soon gained a reputation for a sexual appetite, which was not a positive reputation, so she made it a point to go from city to city, from party to party, club to club; from Maine to South Carolina, from New York to Chicago. Of course, she quit school, and didn't talk to her parents. She'd acquired her trust fund, left by her grandmother, not long after Roland had gone to Europe. It was a sizable amount. It was easy for a young woman with a great deal of money to move comfortably as a nomad. It was the Jazz Age, after all, and she became good at playing the role of a flapper.

When she slept, she did not dream.

It was 1922 and she was twenty-three years old when she found herself at a party at a large mansion near the University of Virginia, at the home of—so she was told—a great writer and historian, Jonathan Blacksmith Caine. She'd gone to the gala with a young man who was studying at the University; she's met him somewhere—she forgot where or how—and slept with him, and was now here with him. The young man—whose name she forgot—was an aspiring writer, and was attending this school because Edgar Allen Poe had been educated here. The only written work by Poe she knew was the poem, "The Raven."

Never more, never more, she said to herself.

She found the party populated by some one hundred or so well-dressed, well-speaking individuals of all ages, extremely boring. The best thing, she decided, was to intake a little cocaine, drink like a fish, and find some fun. She got too drunk, and the young man she came here with took her aside and told her she was embarrassing him.

Fuck you, she laughed: fuck you!

She danced, she laughed, she drank, she propositioned a few men, some who were old and married, but she didn't care.

Everything was spinning. She was taken upstairs by a tall, silver-haired man in a tuxedo. She tried to kiss him.

You've had too much to drink, my dear, he said. I am taking you to bed.

To screw me? she asked.

So you can sleep, he said.

I don't need sleep, she said.

I'm a wise man of many years, so take my advice. Yes, you do need to sleep. Rest the demons inside you, because they need to rest.

You talk funny, she said.

So I've been told, he said.

The man guided her to what she assumed was a guest room—guest rooms always having that certain feel and look about them. He laid her down on the bed.

She pushed her dress up and spread her legs.

I want you, she said.

He looked at her sex and said, That's a very kind offer, and you're a beautiful young woman, but sleep now.

I don't want to sleep, she said.

He closed her eye-lids with warm fingers, and kissed her on the forehead.

116

Sleep, he said.

It wasn't an easy sleep, and sometime later—a minute, an hour, she didn't know—a man came to her in the darkness. He smelled of booze. He got on top of her and fucked her. She wasn't ready and he shoved himself into her and it hurt. It was rough and quick. When he was done, he left, and she went back to sleep.

In the late morning, a maid opened the drapes and let the sun in.

Goddamn, Elizabeth said.

Breakfast is downstairs, the maid said. You can join Mr. Caine if you wish.

She went to the bathroom and looked at herself in the mirror. There was nothing she could do about herself. She washed up a little, and went downstairs. The tall, thin man with silver hair was eating poached eggs and bacon at a long table in the dining room, and reading the paper. He smiled when he saw her, placing the paper down.

Please sit, and eat, he said.

Elizabeth sat across from him. Another female servant poured orange juice and coffee, and asked what she'd like to have for breakfast.

Just some bacon, Elizabeth said.

Bacon?

Yes, perhaps ten strips.

Yes, ma'am.

An unusual meal, the man said.

I like to eat meat, she said.

The man picked up a piece of bacon and took a bite into it. He said, It is quite good.

I'm sorry, Elizabeth said, but who are you and where am I?

The man laughed.

What's so funny?

You drank a lot, he said.

I always drink a lot, she said. I went to a party with some fellow. I guess the party was here. I guess I stayed here. The house belonged to some sort of professor, a man of letters, I was told. Are you that man?

My name is Jonathan Blacksmith Caine, he said.

It's a fine American name, Elizabeth said. I hope you won't be offended if I say I don't know who you are, or what work you are famed for.

That's quite all right, my dear. It's refreshing to be unknown.

I see. Well, I hope you are not as equally offended at what is probably my ghastly sight.

I've had similar mornings, he said. He added, In my youth.

The servant brought a plate of bacon out. Elizabeth was ravenous, and ate quickly.

I remember you taking me to the room, telling me to sleep, she said.

You were causing a scene.

It's what I live for.

You needed to go to bed.

Like a good little girl?

Perhaps.

I'm not good.

There's good in everyone.

I remember asking you to make love to me, she said. You declined, but later you came in and did me.

I assure you, Jonathan Blacksmith Caine said, I did not.

Somebody did. It wasn't a dream. I'm still sore.

Hmm. It could be that someone snuck up to your room during the remains of the party.

Most likely, she said, looking down.

You were making many men, how should I say it?

Just say it, she said.

Aware of your presence, he said.

I apologize if I embarrassed you, she said.

Not at all, he said. I was quite amused, and glad. My parties tend to be somewhat stuffy at times.

I'll say, she said with a mouthful of bacon.

You added a bit of spice, he said.

I've been called spicy.

You haven't told me your name.

Elizabeth.

No last name?

Who needs last names. I'm Elizabeth, just *another* debutante out of control!

She laughed at that.

You're not from here, he said.

No, she said. New Hampshire.

Were you staying with the young man you came here with?

God no.

He's a student of mine. Promising, but not much so.

She said, I have a hotel room. Somewhere in town.

Good, Caine said. I shall have your belongings picked up and brought here.

Why?

Certainly you would wish for a change of clothes, he said. After a nice long bath, I'm certain. Then later, I would like to take you to dinner, and we can talk more.

She nodded, thinking about that.

All right, she said.

She returned to the guest room and drew a bath. A maid came and asked if there was anything she required, and Elizabeth said a bottle of brandy would be nice. The brandy was brought to her, and she sat in the tub for an hour, drinking and thinking about nothing.

Her clothes from the hotel were brought to her, and she chose a dark evening dress, cut low, for dinner.

I rather liked your flapper look, Jonathan Blacksmith Caine said, dressed again in a tuxedo.

I can't always be fashionably questionable, she told him. I *am* capable of being a woman of decorum.

Indeed, he said, holding out his arm. She took his arm, and they went into town for dinner.

It was the nicest and most expensive of restaurants, of course; she didn't expect otherwise. She ordered a steak and he had lobster, and she treated herself to plenty of wine and cognac. She learned that Jonathan Blacksmith Caine was a writer of historical tomes of fiction and fact. Mostly, he wrote of wars, especially the Civil War, and the Colonial Wars, and wars of antiquity in the ages of Egypt and Rome. Sometimes he took the viewpoint of a fictional man, and sometimes he took his own voice as a scholar. His work was renown, and he wasn't ashamed to admit it; young men flocked to him for guidance, as well as the occasional young woman. He was adored by his students at the University.

Perhaps I'll read your books one day, Elizabeth said.

And perhaps not, Caine said.

You must be working on a book about the World War, she said.

I'm always working on a book, he laughed.

It seemed like an empty laugh, she thought.

In the chauffeured car, Elizabeth leaned into him.

I had a pleasant and enjoyable dinner, Mr. Caine, she said.

Call me Jonathan, he said.

Jonathan, she said, touching his leg.

He reached for her face. He kissed her.

He said, I would like to make love to you when we get home, Elizabeth.

All right, she said.

In his bedroom, he ripped her dark dress down the middle, suckling her breasts, grabbing her body.

I'll buy you a new dress, he said.

I have plenty of dresses, she said. Will you get me a drink?

Do you need a drink?

I always need a drink.

He left, and returned with a bottle of scotch. She'd splayed herself naked on the bed for him, touching herself between the legs. He poured her a drink, and undressed, and joined her.

Caine had a lithe, muscular body, but he was an old man, and it showed. The hair on his chest and his pubes were as silver as the hair on his head. His penis was long and thin and curved like a banana. Elizabeth had never seen a penis like that. In fact, it occurred to her she never looked at many men's sex organs, given her encounters; she could tell if the cocks were big or small, thick or thin, when inside her; but she hardly ever saw them. Even when she would perform oral sex, it was often in the dark. But tonight she could take in the details of Cain's cock, the veins, the skin, the way it felt, tasted, and smelled.

He took her, and fucked her for what seemed like a very long time, in several positions. It was several hours at least, and both their bodies were covered in sweat.

Don't you ever come? she asked him.

You want me to come? he said.

I was wondering, she said.

I've been all over the world, my dear, he said. In India, I learned from a Yogi Master on how to control my body, and how to become a lover of stamina. I can make love to you until the sun rises. My body is still in good shape. You need only tell me to climax, and I will.

An hour later, she said: Come inside me.

He did.

And they slept.

She woke several times during the early morning, in his arms, and she went back to sleep. Later, he was not there. She got up, found a white robe waiting for her on the bed. She put it on, went downstairs. She found Caine, in a similar white robe, in the kitchen. He was making breakfast.

Where are the servants? she asked.

They're only here three days a week, he said. I'm not *that* wealthy, and I don't always believe in servants.

We're all alone in this big, big house? she said.

Yes, he replied. I imagine you'd like a lot of bacon strips.

She said, Some eggs, scrambled. Yes. Some coffee, some juice. Can I help? she said.

I enjoy cooking, he said, and I'm almost done.

She went to the main room, found the bar, and had a quick drink of Vodka.

She joined Caine, sitting closer to him at the long table. They had a very nice breakfast. He'd placed ten strips of bacon out for her. Somewhere in the distance, she could hear faint, soft piano music.

Where's that coming from? she said.

The Gramophone, he said.

The music stopped, and they ate. They didn't speak much, and looked at each other.

I'm not a good man, he said, and you must forgive me.

What do you mean?

I'm an old man with dirty thoughts. I have a beautiful young woman in my house, and I see an advantage. I dine you, get you drunk, and make love to you....

What's wrong with that?

Many things.

I had fun, she said.

Fun? he said.

Yes.

He smiled.

They continued to eat breakfast.

I'd like some dessert, Elizabeth said.

I believe I have an apple pie, he said.

That's not what I had in mind, she said, and slid under the table. She crawled to him, opening his robe, taking him into her mouth. He pushed the chair back, so he could watch her, and touch her hair. His long, curved penis grew in her mouth, and she grabbed it at the base. She looked up at him and said, Don't hold back like you did last night. I can't suck for three hours.

He said, All you need to tell me is when, and I will.

Forty minutes later, she asked him to come, and he filled her mouth with several bursts of thick semen. She tried to swallow it all, but it was too much, and some dribbled from her mouth, down his cock, and onto his testicles and the floor. She licked him clean after.

He took her to the bedroom, and gave her oral pleasure for an hour, her legs on his shoulders, her rear raised high, his mouth all over her cunt. She came twice. He turned her on her stomach, entered her, said: yes. He fucked her for several hours until she couldn't take it any more, and she asked him to come, and he did.

They were in each other's arms.

You don't know what a joy this is, he told her.

What?

I'm a man of sixty-three, he said. To be here, making love to a young woman, it's a true dream.

I'm sure you have many eager girls vying for your company, she said.

Occasionally, he said. The women I spend time with are in their thirties or forties. Not so young as you.

I don't believe that.

On occasion, a woman your age. But very seldom.

You're very desirable, she said.

She touched his penis. She took it in her mouth, until he was hard, and got on top of him.

They made love for three hours. She asked him to come, and he did. Their bodies and the sheets were soiled with sweat and sex.

We can sleep in one of the guest's room, he said.

Mine, she said.

They held one another in the guest room, waiting for sleep.

You've been married before, Elizabeth said.

Three times, he said.

Three!

Oh yes.

Three, she whispered, closing in on dreamless sleep.

I've loved too much, he said, I could never love again. Not real love. I can love for the moment, like the moment we spend now. But tomorrow is another day.

I loved once, for one second, she said. Never more, as the raven said.

And they slept.

She spent the next week there, because it felt right, and there was nothing else to do. She ran out of cocaine, and her new lover was not a fan of the drug. So she drank.

It may not be my place to say, he said to her, but you drink an awful lot, my dear.

So I do, she said. So what.

It will catch up on you, he said.

Don't lecture me, she told him.

I shall not, he said.

During the days, she slept, or drank, or lounged outside in the Virginia sun. It was spring. Caine was either at the University teaching his classes, or in his study, doing whatever it was he was doing researching, writing. She didn't know or care. She *did* know it was soon time to go. She wanted to go to New York. She missed New York.

The night she knew she had to leave, Caine had guests, three men near his age, all scholars, writers—one was from Rhode Island, one from California, another from England. She sat across from Caine at dinner. All the servants were here. There was a lot of talk about literature and politics, and Russia and Communism. She wasn't all that interested. She ate her food and drank. And drank. Sometimes she would interject, and all the men would just look at her and smile, like she was a fool. She didn't enjoy that feeling.

In Caine's bedroom, she stood naked, drink in hand, looking at the man lying on the bed, reading an infernal book.

I hate your intellectual crowd, she said.

Why?

Does there need to be a reason?

They are all fine men, Caine said. Did you not find them appealing?

All men are appealing, she said, because they are men.

You're drunk, he said.

Yes, she said. Of course, she said.

He fucked her for two hours.

I needed that, she said. Sex is all I know. Sex is my rhetoric and language.

She laughed.

Good, he said, because I have an assignment for you.

She sat up and said, Oh! An assignment!

Yes, Caine said. You made a good impression on my colleagues. They enjoyed your company, and your sight. I want you to visit each of my guests in their rooms, and fuck them.

All three? she said.

Yes, he said. And come back here, and tell me about it.

All right, she said.

She stood, and looked for something to wear.

Go to them naked, Caine said, so there won't be any question as to why you are there.

First, she visited the man from Rhode Island. He was the youngest, at forty-eight. He was reading, and smiled when he saw the naked young woman enter his room. He fucked her on the bed, and she left, and went to the man from California, who was also awake and reading, and was close to Caine's age, and smiled when he saw the naked young woman. She took him in her mouth, and she got on top of him. The Englishman, in his fifties, was asleep, but awoke when she sat on the bed.

Are you an angel? he inquired.

Hardly, she replied.

He came to his senses, out of sleep, looked at her, and said, Oh.

Hello, she said.

Jonathan is up to his usual tricks, he said.

What tricks?

He laughed and said, Can I have you?

That's why I'm here.

I'd like to fuck you in your bum, he said.

What?

Your arse.

He sodomized her. She'd only done this once, and while she didn't like the first time, this wasn't all that un-pleasant, as it didn't last long.

She returned to Caine's room. He'd lit several candles.

You're back early, he said. It's only been an hour.

They're not like you, she said, they're like regular men.

Tell me, he said, and she told him about each of them.

How do you feel? he asked.

I need a drink.

She had two.

I want to spank you, he said.

Do you?

You've been a bad girl.

I have.

She lay on the bed, and he slapped her rear end with his bare hand many times, until her bottom was red and she had tears in her eyes. Caine stuck a finger into her ass-hole.

My British friend did sodomize you, he said, as Limeys tend to do.

He laughed. She smiled.

Yes, she said.

For the next two hours, Caine fucked her in the ass—his curved penis was an odd sensation until she could take no more, and asked him to come, and he did.

They slept in each other's arms.

In the morning, he woke her.

Leave me alone, she said.

Come have breakfast with us, he said.

Not now, she said.

I insist, my dear.

She got up, looking for her robe.

Remain naked, he said. I want you naked.

She went downstairs, and had breakfast with the four men in the nude. The servants didn't blink an eye. The men seemed to enjoy her like this.

When I first met dear Elizabeth, Caine announced after they ate, she finished her morning meal with my semen in her stomach. Elizabeth?

Yes? she said.

Crawl under the table, and satisfy me, he said.

She did. She went to him under the table, and sucked him, and he came in her mouth.

Now, he said, do the same to each man here.

She went to the man from Rhode Island first, then the one from California, and then the one from England. None of them had washed, and she could taste herself on each. She very much liked this, all their cocks in her mouth, their semen in her mouth. She'd never eaten so much come at once, and her lips and chin were covered in the excess. When she was done, Caine told her to go upstairs. She did. She took a bath, the taste of semen strong on her tongue, and went to sleep.

The three men were gone by evening, and she was once again alone with Caine. She told him how much she enjoyed being a sexual toy like that.

I knew you would, he said.

I've been fucked by several men at once, she said. It was drunk and sloppy; this was different.

Yes, he said, and he fucked her four hours that night.

She remained there for a few more days, and told him she had to go on. New York was calling her.

What's in New York? Caine asked.

I don't know, she said. It's *New York.*

I have nothing to do this weekend, he said. Perhaps I can accompany you? In have friends in New York.

All right, she said.

That weekend they traveled to New York, and they checked into the Waldorf-Astoria, which Caine first thought was excessive, until Elizabeth said she would take care of the bill.

Caine made many phone calls to various people he knew in the city. She lounged in the bath, drinking bourbon.

He came to her and said: We must continue our sexual play.

Yes, she said.

Tell me, my dear, that you will do anything for me.

She said, I will do anything for you.

He pulled her from her bath, took her to bed, fucked her in his usual way, and then opened one of his valises. He had wrist and ankle restraints, and a blindfold. He tied her hands and legs together, and blindfolded her, fed her bourbon and scotch, and left her naked on the bed.

She slept.

He returned, and he wasn't alone. She could smell the other man, he was that strong—his sweat, his cologne.

Caine removed her blindfold and she saw the large black man—he was over six feet tall, in a beige suit and hat, heavyset with large eyes.

This is Jefferson, Caine said as an introduction. A very white name, yes, but a name he has embraced. Jefferson and I go back. He is a poet and writer of stories, although not as well known as he should be. Lives in Harlem, works the clubs to make money. One day I hope to make the world aware of his talent. I've brought him here for you, and for me.

I have to pee, she said.

Jefferson started to take his pants off.

I've brought a number of women to Jefferson, Caine said.

Why? she asked.

To watch, he said matter-of-factly. I absolutely enjoy watching women being defiled by Jefferson.

You want to watch me? she said. I have to pee.

You'll comply? Caine said.

Yes, she said.

Give her some cocaine first, Jefferson said.

Caine nodded, and held the powder to Elizabeth's nose, and also gave her a drink. Every time she asked to have her hands released, and that she had to use the bathroom, Caine smiled and shook his head.

She was told to fellate Jefferson. He had what she assumed must be a deformed cock, by the size of it. It was at least fifteen to sixteen inches long, and very thick and veined and smelly, the bell of the head gargantuan. She could barely get the head of the thing into her mouth! Jefferson stroked himself as she sucked, and Caine sat back and watched, sipping from a drink. Then the black man fucked her, and he was too big, and it was painful. The more she asked him to stop, the harder he fucked her, and she realized she was bleeding from being stretched out so. He tried to put it in her anus, but it wouldn't happen—he got in part way, but she cried for mercy, and then she peed and shat all over the bed. This is some fine stuff, Jonathan, the black man said. She sucked him and he ejaculated into her mouth, a discharge that seemed to last forever, so that she choked on it, spitting his come out, a stream flying from his cock and into her hair. He patted her on the head and both men left. The bed was covered in blood and urine and fecal matter. She didn't care, and went to sleep.

When she woke, she was next to Caine, and the sheets were clean, but she was still in pain. It seemed to be a different room, but she wasn't sure. Her arms and legs were free. She got up, went to the bathroom, and found a bottle of bourbon. She drank, and went to sleep. In the morning, Caine fucked her for a few hours, and they lounged in bed.

Don't ever do that to me again, she said.

I was under the assumption you enjoyed variety, he said.

Not like that, she said. She asked, Did you like watching?

Yes, he said.

I don't like black men, she said.

I wish to arrange one more get-together, Caine said. Nothing extreme. Very ordinary. Very white and upper-class.

All right, she said.

That night, they went to a speakeasy Caine had clout to enter. He wanted her to dress like a flapper, and wear her Egyptian hair-piece, and she did. She held his arm as they entered, and she noticed the eyes on her—the young woman with the older man. She didn't like it at all. She didn't want to be here. She didn't like the eyes. They sat at a table and ordered drinks. There was a jazz band on stage, all black men. She liked the music. She could get good and drunk and dance, like she always did. She needed to get away from Caine. She'd been in his company for almost a month.

Caine spotted two men he knew at a table. They were well-dressed, in their thirties, hair slicked-back, guns under their jackets.

You'll fuck them tonight, he told her, and it'll be nothing like you've ever experienced.

He went to talk to them.

The whole time they'd been here, Elizabeth had been aware of a young man in snappy suit at the bar: his eyes on her. She immediately went to him.

Buy me a drink, she said.

Okay, he said.

Martini. Vodka, shaken, olive.

The young man waved to the bartender.

She downed the drink, fast.

What's your name? she asked.

Gregory, he said.

Let's go, she said.

What?

Gregory, she said.

What? he said.

Let's get *out* of here, she said.

He seemed confused.

Don't you want to take me out of here? she said.

Yes, he said.

Well, she said.

They left, and got into his Model T, and drove.

You were using me, he said.

Everyone uses everyone, she said.

I saw you come in with that man.

I saw you eye-balling me.

You needed to get away, he said.

So what, she said.

Sooooooo what, he said, laughing. You look very familiar. What's your name?

I don't have a name.

I've seen you before.

It's the clothes, the hairpiece, the white make-up, she said. You see me everywhere in this city.

I know you, he said.

No you don't, she said.

They drove.

So what's next? he said.

You have a place? she asked.

Yes.

You want to take me there?

Yes, he said.

Gregory was twenty-five, a Yale grad, and was a stockbroker—she learned this during the drive to his up-town apartment. He was successful, up-and-coming. making money. America was in good shape, and the economy was getting better and better each day, and he was making more and more money every day, as were many people.

It won't last, she said.

It'll last forever, he said.

He took her into his apartment, and they had a drink. He took her to the bedroom, they kissed and undressed, and he fucked her on his unmade bed. It was fast and rough. He put himself into her before she was ready, and it hurt, but he didn't last long. He lit a cigarette and they lay there. He got up, went to the bathroom, and when he came back, he said, Your name is Elizabeth.

She was adjusting her hairpiece. What?

I know you, he said, Elizabeth. You used to be Roland's girl.

She felt cold.

Right? he said.

She said, How do you know Roland?

He was a classmate of mine! You were always with him. You don't remember me?

No, she said, feeling funny.

Well, we only met a few times. But I remember you.

Okay, she said, so you know me.

You were in love with Roland? That's what he said. You were engaged, I think.

What is the point? she said.

I'm sorry, he said. What happened to Roland was tragic.

Oh, she said.

I wanted to go, too. The war. Yes, I did. But my parents wouldn't hear of it. I should've went, he said.

Good for you, she said.

I shudder thinking what his days are like, Gregory said, sitting on the bed. I have no idea what a life like that must mean. He had so much promise.

What the hell are you talking about? she said.

Gregory was stroking himself, smiling. What?

What his days are like? she said. What do you mean?

Don't you ever wonder?

What?

How he lives?

HE DOESN'T LIVE! she cried. HE'S DEAD!

He stared at her. My God, he said.

WHAT?!

You don't know.

Know what?

You really don't know, he said. I heard you

WHAT?? KNOW WHAT?!?

I'm horny, Gregory said. You want to go at it again?

She hit him in the face.

The next day, she took the train to New Hampshire, and a taxi to the home of the young man she once loved. A servant answered, and Elizabeth declared herself. Roland's mother came to the door.

My dear girl, the older woman said, it has been some time. It's nice to....

Let me in, Elizabeth said.

I knew one day you would come, she said. I feared

Why didn't you tell me?

Tell you?

I want to see Roland.

No you don't.

I DO!

Listen, dear girl, Roland's mother said. Your parents and I decided not to tell you. Not at first. We were going to. Then you became wayward, and you disappeared. Elizabeth, honey, your mother and father are worried about you. Call them, right now.

I want to see Roland, Elizabeth said.

No.

YES!

I implore you, Roland's mother said.

Why was I lied to? Elizabeth asked.

I will take you to him, Roland's mother said. They say he can hear, but I'm never certain. He cannot talk to you, he cannot see you. He cannot touch you, or even kiss you. He may hear you. But what you will see, I could never prepare you....

We were going to be married, Elizabeth said. She was crying. She said, He was my love. He was to be my husband. We were going to have children. Goddamn you, you witch, take me to my love!

Forgive me, Roland's mother said. Forgive us all.

They went upstairs, and stopped at a door.

I give you one last chance to turn away, the mother said.

What happened to him?

He walked on a land mine in Belgium, It was war, my dear. A very stupid war.

Elizabeth entered the room, and closed the door behind her. The room was very white. On a bed lay what remained of Roland. It was a body, with no legs and one arm. The body had no discernible face—traces of what used to be a mouth, eyes, nose, and ears. The body twitched, hearing her, maybe smelling her. Whatever this was, she knew it was Roland. She just knew.

Roland, she said, it's me: Elizabeth.

The body twitched.

She sat on the edge of the bed, and the body made more movements.

I've come back, she said,

She looked out the window, and saw two sparrows in a nest, in the tree that loomed over this bedroom.

They told me you were dead, she said.

She pulled the covers away from him. He still had a penis. She took it in her hand, and it grew hard.

I'm not the same girl you knew, she said, but I know more things. I can make you very comfortable and happy.

She got into the bed and lay next to him, stroking his penis. The body twitched like crazy, and the one arm reached over and gently touched her hair.

Hush, my dear, she said, kissing the non-existent lips on what was once a face of a bright young man.

They made love—their bodies—in a way left only to your imagination; and they went to sleep, which was, for Elizabeth, abysmal and full of dreams.

TOYS

After work, I went to Rosina's apartment. Her front door was unlocked, like she had told me it would be. I could hear her in her bedroom, typing away at her computer. She was sitting at her desk in shorts and a halter, hair pulled up in a messy tail.

"Hey," I said.

She spun around in her chair. "You!"

"Expecting someone else?" I sat on the bed.

"Only you. Only you would be here."

"What are you writing?"

"What does it look like?"

I saw a poem on the screen. "What's the subject?"

"Flying. If I had wings," she said, "I could fly. I could fly here, I could fly there. I'd be rich! Everyone in the world marveling at how I can *fly*."

"*I* can fly." I lay back on the bed.

Rosina got on top of me. She tickled me and said, "Can you now?"

"Stop!"

"No."

She stopped.

"I'm a superhero," I told her. "But this is a secret. Well, now you know the secret. When I'm a superhero, I can fly. I'm a superhero with no name."

"Show me," she said. She kissed my nose. "I want to see you fly."

"Can't," I said. "Not in costume. Right now, I'm a regular person."

"But when you're a superhero?"

"I can fly."

"Well," Rosina said, "not *all* of them can."

"Superman does."

"Batman doesn't."

"He doesn't have superpowers. He's a vigilante."

"Batman is *sexy*," and she rolled off me, looking at the ceiling. "I've seen those movies. I'm not talking about the goofy Batman on TV. I mean the movies, *armored-plated nipples and everything*!"

"All superheroes are sexy," I said, bored.

"Does Spiderman fly?"

"No. He swings around the city with his fake webs."

"Who's that guy who runs really fast?"

"The Flash."

She said, "I'd like to be like that, run around all in red, running faster than faster than I don't know what."

I moved to kiss her, to say, "You're Wonder Woman."

She got up. "No. I'm too short, if you have not noticed. So," she bent down, and grabbed my legs, "when you're a superhero, do you wear one of those tight, sexy spandex outfits?"

"You bet."

"And battle evil foes?" Her hands were running up my legs.

"I keep the world safe and clean," I told her.

"Sexy hero," she said, unzipping my pants. She took my cock out, and started sucking on it. She sucked long and slow; I relaxed and allowed myself to enjoy this. I came, but she didn't swallow. She let it go out of her mouth and down my cock. She looked at it. She moved up onto the bed and put her head on my chest. "So where are we going with all this?"

"This?"

"This," she said, touching my stomach, "and this," touching my wet cock, covered in saliva and semen.

"This." I touched her back, her ass.

She turned and kissed my neck, nuzzled it with her face. "You smell good."

"You smell pretty good yourself."

"You always smell like sex," Rosina said. "Is this a good or bad thing?"

"Everything between us is a good thing," I said.

"Everything just seems to be *too* good. We'll end in tragedy," she said.

"Tears?"

"Violence?"

"Pain?"

"Maybe blood," she said. She sat up. "Put your hands here," indicating her neck. She took my hands, and put them around her neck. "There, there. Now choke me."

"Why?"

"I want you to."

"I don't know how."

"Keep your hands there and *squeeze.*"

"Like this?"

"Harder."

"I'll hurt you."

"Just do it, you bastard."

I squeezed her neck. "You like this?"

"You know what I like?" She broke free from me. She plopped down on her hands and knees, body on top of me. She said, "What I really like is for men to fuck me from behind, my ass high in the air, and reach over, here, *here*"—taking my hand—"reach over like so and choke me like so as they fuck me from behind like so."

"Is this romantic talk?"

"Depends on your upbringing," Rosina said.

"Sometimes," I said, "I like the silence."

She put her head on my chest. "Is this getting serious?"

We stopped talking, and started kissing, which led to fucking. I fucked her the way she wanted, my cock in her pussy from behind, and I reached over and choked her. It wasn't an easy thing to do; I thought it'd be easier if she were on her back, I'd have better access to her neck. "Choke me harder," she pleaded, and I did, and her body shook as she came, my hand still at her neck. "Oh boy," she said.

* * * * * * *

I began to enter Rosina's world of pain: her delight.

I was touching, caressing her breasts. I pinched her nipples, which were hard; I pinched lightly.

"Pinch them harder," she said.

I did.

"Harder," she said.

I was afraid I'd hurt her.

"I want the pain," she said. "It makes me horny."

She gave an example. She got up, found a pair of clothespins in a cabinet in the kitchen, and placed a clothespin on each nipple. With the clamping down on each nipple, she took in a deep, hissing breath.

"Fuck," she said.

"You like that," I said.

"Yes, yes," she said. "Take them off."

I did, quickly.

"Put them back on."

I did, and this time I took delight in watching the pins squeeze into her flesh.

"Ahh, fuck," she said.

I took one off.

"Now use your fingers."

I took the nipple in question between two fingers.

"Squeeze," she said.
I squeezed.

* * * * * * *

I started to become quite good at choking her while we fucked, whether she was on her belly or on her knees or stomach. Repetition makes you better. I also started to enjoy this activity. I was never quite sure if it was mental or physical for Rosina, but as long as it got her off and made her happy, it made me happy.

We started biting one another, soft at first, then harder, sometimes until we drew blood from each other's punctured flesh, fragile as anything in the universe. The biting was not just into the body, but into the soul.

"I have something," Rosina said, standing naked before me.

"Yeah?"

"Something I want you to use on me," she said.

She went to her closet, and produced a cat-o'-nine-tails. I'd seen such a flogging device in magazines, in movies.

"Where'd you get that?" I asked.

"I've had it awhile," Rosina said. "I want you to use it on me," she said.

It was black and ominous. She handed it to me. She lay on her stomach, on the bed. "Use it on my back," she told me. "Use it on my ass, my legs."

I did so, lightly, uncertain.

"It's okay to start off soft," she said, "but increase your strength. Gradually. I want you to get to a point where you could almost make me bleed."

I did this. I hit her with the cat-o'-nine-tails just as she said: her back, her ass, her legs. She seemed to like it best on her ass. I started to get into it. I started hitting her harder, enjoying the smack of leather against flesh.

Harder. She began to cry out with each blow. Tears in her eyes. She wanted more. Welts were beginning to form on her ass, the backs of her legs. I concentrated on her back, 'til welts formed there.

"Okay," she said. *"Stop."*

I stopped. I, too, was almost out of breath.

"Now get on me," she said. "Fuck me, I can't stand it, fuck me!"

I entered her from behind, I reached over to choke her. We fucked for a bit, then she turned around and put her legs on my shoulders.

"Slap me," she said.

I raised a hand.

"Slap me."

Fucking her, I slapped her, hard, across the face.

She just looked at me, some blood on her lip. "Not that hard," she said.

"I'm sorry," I said, reaching down and licking the blood away.

"Slap me again," she said.

I did, but not as hard.

* * * * * * *

Rosina bought toys several days a week, usually at thrift stores, sometimes at the toy store. She loved her children's toys.

But she had adult toys hidden under her bed, and it wasn't until we'd been seeing each other for a month that she brought them all out, and wanted to share them with me.

Anal beads, large double-headed black dildos, a dog collar, other assorted rubber penetrating devices. While Rosina liked the beads or my fingers in her ass, she didn't care for anal sex all that much. She wasn't into ass-licking, piss, or even swallowing my come. She liked pain, she liked to whack her clit off, she liked me to choke her. It was easy to get into what she enjoyed, as I got into any woman's pleasure, however alien it was to me. I adapted well.

* * * * * * *

The image I have of her—this image will always stay with me—is of Rosina surrounded by her toys, a milieu of toys: the toys she liked to buy and play with, fill the empty spaces of the apartment with.

This is what I knew about her—or this could've been mere assumption—and the image of her that sticks like hot glue to the fingertips of my reverie is Rosina as I saw her one night, when I went to her apartment and she had bought a bag full of magnetic letters, the colored alphabet letters I seem to recall having played with when I was a very small person. "Look! Look!" she said with glee, like a small person, and she said, "Help me with them," an invitation to play. She tore open the plastic bag the colored letters were contained in; they scattered across the floor of her kitchen like stupid human dreams forever lost in a car crash. She went to her knees, told me to come to her: play, help, fight. She started putting the letters on the white refrigerator, where she had a color print of a happy smiley-face woman with large eyes and the caption HOME HONEY, I'M HIGH and two postcards, one of a brunette holding a gun and shooting, another of a man with a gun, an image from the movie *Reservoir Dogs*. There was a mixture of delight and anxiety on her face; she looked at me and said, "Won't you help me?" I got to my knees, picked up several letters, started putting them on the fridge with her. The kitchen was hot (like the rest of the apartment) and I felt very sad. She must've seen something on my face because she said, "You think this is silly, you don't like doing this."

"No," I said, "there's nothing silly about this," and so we were like two children frantically picking up the alphabet from her floor—letters that I thought would any moment now get up and dance—sticking them to the door of the fridge. Merriment, yes, a small one's joy on her small triangular face; and when I looked at the kitchen table that held a lot of other toys, used and new, I felt sad again; I knew there was something missing. Something was missing from her past (something was missing from mine) and something was missing between us, yet another space to be filled, a vacuous interior needing intestines.

"You buy so many toys," I said. I sat down at the table and played with a dinosaur.

Rosina looked at her letters, arranged them in a way she liked better. "Yes, I do," she said.

She sat in my lap like she always did, arms around my neck and looking down at me with her dark eyes, dark circles under her eyes—my face pressed against her breasts, the smell of her now on me, that smell that was not perfume but some men's cologne I'd never heard of that mixed well with her skin and gave her the smell I knew I'd forever associate with her, an invasion of my psyche: my memory of Rosina.

She kissed me on the lips, she kissed me on the forehead. "Just think," she said, "I keep collecting more and more toys, we'll never have to buy toys for our children."

* * * * * * *

One night at her apartment I felt, for the first time, like I did not belong there. I was feeling weak. All day I had had this sensation of horror, but all I wanted was to be with her, to hold her, to have her hold me, to play with her toys, to talk, to have her warm body against mine, to make love, to do anything, anything but be away from her; whip her, slap her, beat her, choke her. Her apartment was dark, candles were lit all around, flamenco guitar music on the CD player. She was in the bathroom, hair pinned up, applying makeup in a way she never had before, looking at herself in the mirror; and when I went into the bathroom, her eyes on me, from the reflection, were eyes of rancor. She seemed angry, like she didn't want me there; she seemed evil in the candlelight. I tried to kiss her and she pushed me away. Once, she told me she did a lot of symbolic things, some abstruse and some subtle, and I would have to get used to it. "Like this band on my wedding finger," she said, "is to remind me who and what I'm really married to: *myself*, I'm married to myself; and this necklace, these earrings in the shape of hearts, to remind me to always follow my heart."

"Why are you here with me?" she had asked after we made love the night before. "I don't understand," she said.

I grabbed her necklace and said, "I'm just following my heart."

In the candlelit apartment she told me she was having second thoughts; she wasn't sure if she wanted a partner, someone to tell her to come to bed at four a.m. while she was working on a poem; someone to tell her to eat; someone to even talk to, to be present for, to remind herself of herself. "I'm used to being a hermit," she said. "I like being a hermit." I told her I would go but she grabbed me and said no and we held each other and I smelled her and I was all the more confused.

* * * * * * *

I saw her touching herself, making herself come, the way she liked to, lying on her stomach, and how hard she did this to herself, finger to clit. When I tried doing it to her, I never seemed to do it hard or fast enough. "Press, press," she said, her body drenched in light, sweet-smelling sweat.

144

As I saw her masturbating, the image was replaced again by that of her on the kitchen floor, picking up the alphabet, playing with her toys.

Yes, it was over and I would live with this hole in my heart forever, and I'd never look at toys the same way again.

TWO GIFTS

I never thought much about sex during the holidays; it was Christmas Eve and Erin was supposed to come by after her show; it was closing night of a play she was in and we were going to meet for a few drinks and talk about our lives. I hadn't seen her in two years; she was in a play I had written and directed, back when I was doing theater. She was an actress among the many local actresses in the local theater scene. There was something between us once, the back and forth, casually sleeping together, brief discussions of getting together, then silence, then nothing: more collected memories of scenes that could never match.

We started emailing again; she was still single, a single mother, working a nine-to-five office job and doing theater at night and dreaming the things all hopeful actresses dream of. I found myself greatly looking forward to seeing her; I had visions of us picking up where we left off, recreating some sense of hope and love, and waking up together on Christmas morning, each renewed like Ebenezer, cheerful music playing in the background—hark the angels sing and all that—and her daughter like Tiny Tim, telling us all is well, God bless. And then everything would be okay. But her daughter wasn't with her this Christmas, she was in some other state with her father, and I knew Erin was depressed and lonely because the only person who mattered to her was away from her on this cold C. Eve. It was so chilly I could see my breath form smoke in my apartment and I was wearing gloves. I had presents for her and her kid—last minute items that I went out and bought and had wrapped because I felt it was something to do, something I had to do. It made me feel good to buy these gifts and what was better: it made me feel something.

She came by after her show—she said it was a good closing night, with half the house filled, which isn't bad for a closing—and we walked down the block to a neighborhood bar.

There were maybe seven people in the bar, some playing pool, some sitting around. We both had white Russians. I got up to go to the bathroom, was gone maybe thirty seconds, and there was already a guy sitting next to her at the counter—he was playing pool—acting like he was going to order a drink. Twenty empty seats at the counter and he sits on the one next to hers?

"Excuse me," I said.

He turned to me.

"Um."

I nodded at my drink.

He looked at my drink, then me, his eyes red, angry, like he wanted to hit me. I was ready for anything. He moved away and there was no incident.

Erin grinned. "I haven't been inside a bar in a year. I forget what it can be like."

"Has he been waiting for me to go take a piss to make his move?"

"I've been on dinner dates when my date gets up for the restroom, men sitting at other tables immediately introduce themselves with flattering words. 'Oh, I just want to say, what a nice dress...your hair is very nice, I like your shoes.'"

"Jerks."

"People are lonely everywhere," she said.

We had a second drink and left the bar. Outside, a girl in a thick jacket, straight black hair and heavy eyeliner asked if we had any spare change.

"No," said Erin.

I gave the girl a dollar.

"Thanks, man!" said the girl.

"I never give anyone change," Erin said.

"It's Christmas," I said.

"Yeah: ho, ho."

Back at my apartment, she didn't want to come inside, she wanted to go home, so I tried to kiss her and she kissed me back but said softly, "Did you think something was going to happen?"

I didn't know how to answer that.

"I just wanted to drop bye, say hi, have a drink," she said.

"Of course," I said.

She left. I went inside and looked at the gifts. She called from her cell. "I'm sorry about that," she said.

"It's okay."

"It's not okay."

"You could come back."

"Some things have happened," she said. "I'm just not into that right now…."

* * * * * * *

I didn't have any booze at home. I went back to the bar. There was still an hour before last call.

The girl with the black hair and thick jacket was still outside, asking for change.

"Hey," she said, "thanks for the dollar again!"

"Want a drink?"

"What?"

"Do you drink?"

"Who doesn't?"

"Wait; you old enough?"

She laughed. "Funny. I'm twenty-five!"

I had another white Russian and she had a Long Island Iced Tea and then we had two more. She said her name was Taylor and I didn't believe her. She said she was sleeping in her car tonight, as she had been all week. She didn't go into details and I didn't need them.

"I live a block away," I said.

"I can't give it you for free," she said after a pause.

"I know."

"Just to get that out of the way."

Back at my apartment, I asked her how much.

"Um," Taylor said, rolling her eyes. She was nervous. "Let's see. Okay, look, I don't really do this so I'm not sure what the going rate is, you know, for a blowjob or a fuck or if you want to stick it in my ass."

"How about everything?"

"How about $100."

"Deal."

"That was easy."

"I like it when it's easy."

I got out my wallet and handed her five $20s. She rolled them up and the money disappeared in her jacket like she was a magician.

In bed, her body was taut and slender from too many missed meals—that thick jacket hid how skinny she really was. Her skin was pale and goose-bumped. I held her close to me, under the blankets, until she seemed to get warm.

We kissed.

"This is nice," she said, like she was surprised.

"Yeah."

"Condoms?"

"Plenty," I said, reaching for the nightstand drawer, where I had a dozen assorted brands.

"Always prepared," she said.

"Always hopeful," I said.

We fucked for a while, this position and that, she was responsive and moaning; while I had her on her stomach, she said softly, "Okay, now, stick it my asshole."

"Yeah?"

"You paid for it, boy."

"Do you want that?"

"It's what I want, now," she said, her voice changing, deeper, *"now, stick it in, motherfucker, just do it."*

I did and she went limp and purred.

* * * * * * *

She started to get dressed.

"Where you going?"

"A question filled with mystery and no answers," she said.

"Don't sleep in your car. You can stay here."

* * * * * * *

It was 7:00 A.M. and I woke up to a blowjob. It was nice to open my eyes and see a woman with my cock in her mouth. She grabbed a condom from the nightstand and moved on top of me. "Ho, ho, ho," she said.

* * * * * * *

This time she said she really had to go when she put her clothes on. I was going to suggest breakfast but she looked a lot different in the morning light. She appeared scared and confused and I knew she didn't do this much, if ever at all; I knew she felt ashamed and I wanted to tell her not to be.

I walked her to the door.

"Wait," I said.

I picked up the two wrapped presents and handed them to her.

"Happy holidays," I said.

She didn't know what to make of this. "For me?"

"Of course."

"How…?"

"I just knew."

"Thank you," she said, and left.

I felt ashamed, but I was glad the presents were gone.

FEELING SOMETHING

1.

Jordin Bennett was skanky and aloof; she was sitting down in front of her laptop, naked, to finish her first novel one hot day in the middle of July, the Los Angeles smog seeping into the apartment like a midnight intruder bent on ravaging and pillaging unsuspecting virgins.

It was a dreadful, muggy summer in southern California; even with two fans pointed her way, and no clothes, Jordin sweated copiously as she searched for the right words to tell her story.

She was twenty-eight and knew she had to publish (let alone finish) her first novel before she turned thirty...or else she'd never obtain that goal: to be a hot young writer full of promise and aplomb.

Her novel was a romance of sorts, about a threesome. It was generally autobiographical, as most first novels tend to be. She didn't know what to title it, though.

2.

Why, you ask, do I describe Jordin as "skanky"? It's a word she often used herself, joking, "I'm such a skank" and "I do the skanky thang." Her last boyfriend, when breaking up with her, said, "I hate your skanky ass." He was referring to her job as a topless dancer and not her buttocks.

According to *Wikipedia.com*, "skank is slang and a pejorative term used in the Western World to describe a person, usually female, who is either sexually promiscuous in a tasteless manner or behaves in a way which others perceive to be such. The term 'skank' differs from that of 'slut' in that whereas the latter implies only sexual promiscuity, the former also implies poor taste, personally degrading behavior and low socioeconomic class."

Jordin had two dozen assorted tattoos from her neck to her feet; on her arms, back, lower back, ass, hip, fingers and toes. She also had long dreadlocks, the result of two years not washing her red hair.

As for aloof, she *was* aloof. According to the *Merriam-Webster Online Dictionary*, the adjective aloof means "removed or distant either physically or emotionally." Jordin would agree with that. She hadn't felt an authentic emotion in a very long time; she was beginning to wonder if she was an actual human being. All her smiles were faked; when she laughed in public, it was an effort because she felt it was expected of her. She didn't know when the last time she cried was; she didn't remember what it felt like to be in love.

By writing an untitled erotic romance novel, she was hoping to rediscover what she had lost...

3.

In the first chapter of the novel in question, Jordin's heroine, Dominique Speer, is a twenty-four-year-old architectural student living in Santa Monica, California (Jordin herself lived in Burbank). Dominique is an average girl with a dark complexion and long black hair with tints of natural red; she could appear sexier if she dressed differently—she had the body but had negative body-image issues, so she shied away from short skirts or tight jeans. Dominique is depressed because the guy she's been with since she was eighteen, whose name is Brandon Albert, has become far more aloof than the author; he's distant and uninterested in sex or love or the future and she fears the end of the relationship is around the corner like a drunk driver speeding his way to vehicular manslaughter. The novel opens with Dominique sitting in her apartment late at night, watching a David Lynch movie and masturbating to memories of better times with Brandon, when he was a confident young artist and working hard at his paintings and drawings. She is unaware that she is being watched; there is a man standing by her window and peeking through a crack in the blinds. He can see her by the light of her TV, and he can see her hand wandering between her legs. He is touched by the expression on her face when she comes. He falls in love. He waits and watches. Dominique goes to sleep around midnight. He makes his way around the back of the apartment and finds the kitchen window open. He uses a pocketknife to cut through the screen, and then crawls through the window; he's cautious and quiet and he has a history of breaking into people's homes—only to steal things, not to rape. He has no intention of raping Dominique—this is what he tells her when she wakes up, and this is true.

Dominique opens her eyes at 12:25 A.M. and can smell the intruder; his body has the odor of stale sweat, cigarettes, and the street. She sees his silhouette standing near her bed. She sits up.

Hush, he says.

She wants to scream, but she cannot. She wants to get up and run, but she is frozen.

He sits down next to her. He's as nervous as she is.

I'm sorry, he says, I have never done anything like this, but I saw you through the window and you looked like an angel, a beautiful angel, and I had to come in and touch you.

He touches her shoulder.

Her body is shaking; she feels like she might vomit.

I won't hurt you, he tells her; I won't do anything against your will. I just wanted to talk to you, to see you. I won't rape you or kill you, if that's what you're thinking.

She asks, Promise?

Yes, he says.

Let's shake on it, she says.

He shakes her hand and she doesn't let go of it, which is twice the size of hers. She thinks that if she keeps his hand with hers, he can't use it to hurt her. She doesn't believe his promise; she doesn't even know his name.

Nothing bad happens. He lies on the bed with her, holding her hand, and they talk. He does most of the talking. He tells her how he and his girlfriend drove out from South Carolina to L.A. in search of fame and fortune in the music business. He's a keyboard player and the girlfriend is a singer, but she leaves him for another man, a man with money, two weeks after the move. He's been in L.A. for a year, playing a few gigs, not making much cash, living in his car right now.

She tells him about Brandon. She doesn't tell him there are problems. She says: I've been with him for six years and I love him very much.

Where is he now?

Out of town. He's usually here.

I'm jealous, the intruder says, he has you and I don't.

He moves to kiss her. He kisses her on the forehead.

It is six A.M. The sun is starting to come up.

I should go now, he says. He gets up and hands her a $5 bill—for the window screen, he says.

Thank you, she says. You didn't tell me your name.

My name is Life, he says.

4.

To pay the rent, bills, and eat, Jordin worked three or four shifts a week at The Happy Room, a topless dance club in West Hollywood, in the heart of Thai Town. A shift was four to six hours; on a good night, she could make $300-400 in tips and lap dances—on a slow night, $150-200. It was an easy job. Jordin loved to dance; she loved to dance in front of men; she loved to take her top off and show her tits to strangers. Maybe *love* isn't the right word since she was *aloof*—she didn't mind doing it, and it was better than working in an office or retail.

She thought about her character, Dominique, and how Dominique was slowly losing her emotional core after the incident with the trespasser named Life. In the second chapter, Dominique tells Brandon about it. Brandon's response is: I don't believe you. She tells him the story again and he believes her but instead of holding her and assuring her everything will be all right, he becomes even more indifferent and distant than he was before.

Dominique is not Jordin, if that's what you are guessing; that part of the novel is not autobiographical. It is based on a real incident, however; it happened to one of the dancers at The Happy Room, whose stage name is Mecca.

Jordin's stage name is Lira, by the way.

5.

Mecca (real name Shannon O'Hannon) was twenty-nine and had been working as a dancer since she was nineteen, from Phoenix to Seattle to Portland to San Diego and now L.A. She was writing a screenplay about her experiences.

One day, a writer named Michael was in The Happy Room and paid for a few lap dances from Mecca. She asked him what line of work he was in. He told her he was a staff writer for a hit TV show, and had written and directed a couple of independent features that were ignored and lost.

"Really," said Mecca, "I'm writing a screenplay!"

"Isn't everyone?"

"What?"

"You know the three spit Hollywood joke," Michael mused, "spit in the air around Wilshire and Santa Monica, and you'll hit an actor. Spit again and you'll hit an agent. Spit a third time and you'll hit a lawyer. All three of them are trying to sell a screenplay they wrote."

Mecca wanted to pick his brain for information about the business; she managed to talk him into inviting her to dinner. After steak and a baked potato and a few drinks, she gave him a sloppy blowjob in his car. Three months later, they were seeing each other twice a week, so it was some kind of relationship.

Dancers and strippers have a hard time keeping boyfriends. At first the men act like it's cool and okay to date a woman who takes off her clothes in front of anyone and gives dirty old men lap dances...eventually they all grow jealous and that's the end of that.

6.

There is a Michael in Jordin's novel, but everyone calls him Mike. Mike shows up in chapter three. He's a longtime friend of Brandon's, and he is also a writer—a novelist and journalist, not a TV scribe. He's never cared much for Dominique, found her to be snooty and uptight. Dominique calls him one night, asking if he knows where Brandon is.

Don't know, Mike says.

She asks: Is he with another woman? Does he have someone else?

Don't know, Mike says.

Because she has no one to talk to and needs to talk about the man called Life, she tells Mike her story. He listens. He is touched. She sounds sincere on the phone. Mike realizes she is a human being with deep fears and emotions. He likes this.

The two start talking a lot on the phone, then meeting for drinks. He asks if he can kiss her and she says okay. He tells her he wants to sleep with her, but she is afraid, because there is still Brandon....

7.

Mecca wasn't working the night Jordin stepped away from her novel and went to do a shift at The Happy Room—but she was there at the club, with Michael, and they had a bottle of very expensive tequila that Michael claimed he stole from some high-powered TV exec's party.

"I deserve this bottle," Michael said, "for all the changes he's made in my scripts, turning gold into shit, which in the end makes good television, I guess."

8.

At this point you may be wondering if either Michael or Mike are really me, your humble narrator, or perhaps both are based, in part or whole, on yours truly. Consider this: Michel is a fictional character in an unpublished novel and Mike is a real person in Los Angeles. I'll leave the rest to your imagination.

9.

In chapter four of Jordin's novel, Brandon starts to realize that something is going on between his old friend Mike and his estranged girlfriend Dominique. He doesn't care. While drinking beers and eating tacos at a Mexican restaurant one night, Brandon tells Mike to feel free to fuck his girlfriend. She needs it, he says.

You're serious, Mike says.

She seems to be happier lately, because she has you to talk to.

I've been thinking….

Yeah?

You'll be okay with it?

Sure.

You won't change your mind and get mad?

Nah.

You don't love her anymore?

I still love her; just don't want to be intimate with her.

Why?

I'll tell you something, Brandon says, for the past three years, whenever we have sex, I don't come. I can't come. It's not physical. I come when I jack off. I just can't with her. I fuck her for hours and hours and nothing pours out of my dick or my balls. Why? I've realized she repulses me….

(Dominique later tells Mike that she didn't like being fucked for those extended periods of time, she would get sore and bored and felt insulted that Brandon wouldn't reach orgasm. Also, she said, he doesn't like blowjobs, he won't let me go down on him, and I really like having a cock in my mouth.)

It's the same with the dick-smoking, Brandon says; I like a BJ like any other guy, but not from her. Not that she's bad, she's good, I remember her being good, but whenever she gets her face in my crotch, I feel like I want to puke.

Wow, Mike says.

Sucks, Brandon says. I don't mean her, he adds with an empty chuckle.

You know what would be good, Mike says, sad about the uncomfortable situation, is for the three of us to have a threesome.

Why would that be good?

You'll appreciate her more, if you watched another man fuck her.

Hmm, says Brandon, I'll have to think about that...

10.

Mecca and Michael shared the tequila with Jordin. It was the best tequila she'd ever had—it was so smooth it went down like water and didn't burn. The only problem was: Jordin wasn't a drinker, and she quickly found herself inebriated, snookered, smashed, shit-faced and three sheets to the wind. She was so drunk she couldn't dance on the stage. She started to cry in front of the customers. The other dancers and management were not happy in The Happy Room. The doorman/bouncer grabbed Michael by the collar and said: "I should break your fingers for doing that to her!"

"Hey!" Mecca said, slapping the bouncer on the head, "he didn't do anything, it's not his fault, she's an adult, she knows what she's doing!"

Jordin was sitting on the floor, bawling her eyes out, mumbling how hard things were, how she felt nothing, how she was going nowhere, how she was afraid of failing if she didn't publish her first novel before age thirty.

"She's your responsibility then," said the bouncer. "Get her out of here. And don't let her drive."

"Let's take her back to your place," Mecca told Michael; he lived two blocks away from the club.

11.

In chapter six, Dominique is agreeable to a threesome, much to the surprise of both Michael and Brandon. The idea turns her on more than she wants to admit—the *idea*, in theory, that is, because she isn't sure if she can actually go through with it when the time comes, but she wont know until that time arrives like an Amtrak train at Union Station.

She wants this to happen in neutral territory, and suggests a motel room. She also says going out of town would be good.

So in chapter seven of Jordin's book, the three of them drive out to Palm Springs to do the deed. It is an hour and half journey from L.A. to the desert getaway; it is awkward condition. There is tension. There is uncertainty. Brandon is uncomfortable. Dominique is nervously excited. Mike wants to fuck. They talk about trivial things, not about sex or what is going to happen that night.

Next is chapter eight: the three have arrived in Palm Springs and check into one of the many motels on the main drag. More and more, it seems that Brandon is not keen on the whole thing.

I'll go get some booze, Brandon says.

Booze would be good, Mike says.

White Russians! Dominique says.

Brandon leaves. He's gone for a while. Mike and Dominique sit on the bed and start kissing. He reaches under her skirt and touches her; she has thick pubic hair, which is different because most women shave most, if not all, of it off these days; he sticks two, then three fingers inside her pussy, which is very, very wet. This is the first time she has let him go that far. You make me so juicy, she says, I've never been this way before.

She comes twice. The second time she squirts. It's nice and messy.

That's the best hand job I've ever had, she says.

How many have you—?

Not enough, she admits.

Brandon returns, catches them kissing. He stops and stares and looks hurt. He can smell her pussy in the air and knows something happened while he was out.

Hey, Mike says.

Brandon has bought a fifth of vodka, a half-gallon of milk, and a bottle of Kahlua. There are no cups, though.

I'll get cups, Brandon says, and leaves quickly.

He's backing out, Dominique says.

He'll be okay, Mike says; he wanted to do this.

I want to do this, she says, and they start to kiss again....

12.

At Michael's apartment, Jordin stopped crying and wanted more tequila. "Are you sure?" Mecca asked. Jordin grabbed Mecca and kissed her. This wasn't the first time these two had been close. Lesbian encounters among the dancers at The Happy Room, or any stripper club, were commonplace. "Kick back and watch the show," Jordin told Michael. He did. He witnessed the two girls undress, get on his bed, make out and go down on each other. Then he joined them....

13.

Brandon returns with plastic cups and Mike makes them White Russians to drink. He tells Brandon to relax and Brandon says: I am relaxed. In chapter nine, Jordin decides to turn up the heat, the romance, the depravity. *It's time to pork*, she thinks as she types away on the laptop, half-way through her novel now. The three are on the bed. Mike starts to undress Dominique. She's shy at first, but gives in. She keeps looking at Brandon, urging him to be aggressive. Come here and rip my bra off, she says. Mike agrees—tear her panties off, Mike says. Brandon is rubbing one of Dominique's legs, but he can't move. He can only stare. He doesn't believe he is here, that he agreed to this, that he is going to allow his long time buddy to hump his long-term girlfriend.

I've read Paul Bowles and Henry Miller, he says softly; I'm hip.

What's wrong, baby? Dominique inquires, her voice soft with the pain of six thousand years of hurt women.

This is what we came here for, Mike says, somewhat annoyed.

Brandon stands up. He says: You two go for it. I'll watch.

What? Dominique says.

I'll watch.

Mike says: Why don't you draw us…

Good idea, Brandon says. He gets his sketchpad and sits on the floor and says: Go ahead and do what you want, I'll draw.

Fuck it, says Dominique, fuck him, she says and looking at Brandon she adds: Fuck you, you coward, you Nancy boy, you impotent fuck, I'm going to suck cock and take it up my dirty asshole like you've never seen porn before.

Hey, hey, Mike says, holding her.

Just *fuck* me, she says, and make it good.

14.

Mecca woke up first, in bed with Michael and Jordin—who were both cuddling and spooning and lightly snoring. Mecca didn't care for that sight. She got out of bed, put her clothes on, and left. Before departing, she stopped and turned to the two sleeping bodies and muttered, "I hate you people."

15.

Chapter ten has Brandon trying to draw the sex before his eyes. He can't do it. The motel room fills up with the smell of fuck and all he can do is look at the floor. He peeks up now and then, but it's too much –- to see them go down on each other; to see Mike stick fingers in Dominique's ass and have her lick those fingers; to observe them do the sixty-nine position while she faces Brandon, stares at him the whole time, eat Mike's semen and says to him: *I love it when a man comes in my mouth.*

He begins to weep, and then there is chapter eleven, the next morning....

16.

Jordin woke up and freaked out. She had no idea where she was or how she got there. She was in bed with a man she didn't know and could only assume the worst. Michael woke up and said: Hey.

She punched him in the face and jumped out of the bed, naked. She looked around for her purse, found it, grabbed it, and took out the switchblade she always kept for protection.

17.

In chapter eleven, the drive back to L.A. is very un-comfortable. Brandon refuses to talk to either Mike or Dominique. They drop him off where he works and he walks away, not saying goodbye. He is disgusted, but not with them—with himself. Mike and Dominique get lunch, go back to her place, and cuddle in her bed. The hell with him, she says, I want more sex.

Chapter twelve: lots of sex scenes, with some ro-mance.

Chapter thirteen: Dominique tells Mike she loves him. He says it is too soon.

Chapter fourteen: Brandon tells Mike he is okay with everything, even though he is not. He keeps his jealousy buried deep.

Chapter fifteen: Mike has a one-night stand with an eighteen-year-old hottie. He tells Dominique about it and she gets very upset. He goes: We're not in a committed re-lationship, you can go out and screw any guy you want and it wouldn't bug me.

Chapter sixteen: Dominique shows up at Mike's home, drunk. She is holding a bottle of cheap, foul tequila. She demands to know why Mike does not love her. Mike says he could love her, but it's too soon. Dominique strips all her clothes off and says: Is this body good enough for you? Mike reaches out to her and says: I will make love to you. She throws the tequila bottle down, smashes it on the floor, falls down and starts to roll over the glass, cutting herself. She crawls to him, bleeding. *This* is my passion, she says.

18.

Jordin tried to stab Michael with her blade. She chased him around his apartment, screaming she would get even for his taking advantage of her.

Michael pleaded for her to stop, not hurt him, not cut him, not stab him. He said it wasn't like that, he didn't abuse her, he didn't do anything wrong. He said, "Don't you remember last night, when Mecca and I came into The Happy Room with the tequila?"

Jordin stopped, holding the knife in the air like a magic wand, like she was a character in a J. K. Rowling book.

She started to remember....

"Oh no," she said, "oh God, I'm sorry...."

She sat on the bed and sobbed, hands covering her face.

"I'm sorry," she said. "What have I done...?"

He sat next to her and held her.

"It's okay," he said.

She leaned into his chest and wept even more...she grabbed him hard and asked him to forgive her.

"It's all right."

"I finally *feel* something," Jordin said, "I feel real."

And so, she had the title to her novel now.

HOW TO HAVE AN AFFAIR

THE RULES

Wait at least an hour, maybe two, for your wife to fall sleep before going out to see the other woman. The wife usually hits the bed around ten or eleven P.M.; she has to get up early and work at the office. She has adjusted her life, years ago, with your nocturnal habits; you like to work at night behind the computer, writing genre novels (westerns, men's action-adventure) for book packagers under various "house names." Because your wife sleeps, as they say, "like the dead," it's easy for you to slip out of the house for a few hours, return at two or three in the mornings, and she never has a clue you've been gone.

When you're certain the wife is quite asleep, call the other woman on her cell-phone. The other woman's husband is a doctor so he's often away, and that marriage is strained as it is, she keeps saying she'll leave the doctor. She waits impatiently for your call. "God I need to see you bad," she says.

There are two ways you meet her, depending how much time she can get away, (1) she'll drive her car over, park a block away, you'll walk to her car, and the two of you will do your affair thing quickly in the backseat like a couple of kids sneaking sex in the dangerous night; or (2) you will walk two blocks to a cheap motel by the freeway on-ramp, call her cell and inform her of the room number, engage in some quality hours. Either way, you return home, the wife hasn't stirred, you get some work done, you go to sleep around four or five in the morning; you sleep "like the dead" yourself when the wife gets up at seven-thirty to shower, dress, and make way for the office.

This goes on for six months or so; you never get caught but there's always that possibility, *that thrill.* You could lose everything here. Your wife would leave you in the dust if she ever found out.

The other woman really doesn't care if her husband, the doctor, ever finds out.

"I'm not in love anymore, what does it matter," she says.

"He'd be hurt."

"I don't think so. Maybe I should tell him."

"No," you say, "don't tell him."

"You're right," she says, "I *do* want some money when the time comes for a divorce."

I DON'T EVER WANT TO SEE YOU AGAIN

The other woman eventually leaves the doctor and rents an apartment five blocks from your house. It makes things easier for a while, but after a month she lets you know she *really* wishes you could spend the night. "I want to wake up with you in my bed," she goes. This just is not possible. You try getting up after your wife goes to work and returning to the other woman's apartment, but this is simply exhausting. The other woman is worried you have sex with your wife the same nights you have sex with her. "That's crazy," you say, although you have committed this sin on several occasions because let's face it, you're a bad man.

One night, the other woman expresses her dislike at being the mistress, although you've never thought of her as such, and asks: "Do you love me?"

168

"I love my wife, I can't love two"

"Get out!" she says. "I don't ever want to see you again."

It's raining. You feel terrible. You do love her, so you call her from a payphone and, dripping wet, are prepared to tell the other woman that you're scared because you love two women with equal passion and could there ever be a true future in that but the other woman doesn't give you a chance to bare your ugly soul, she says: "Come back. I don't care if you don't love me, I love you, I need you, it's really all about sex, right? The sex is good so come back and fuck me, okay?"

SCENT OF THE OTHER WOMAN

In time, you get caught; anyone who ever has an affair for an extended period will eventually be caught. One night you come home at three in the morning and your wife is awake, sitting on the couch and drinking a drink.

"Oh," you say.

"Where have you been?" she says.

"I went out for a walk," you say, "I needed to clear my head."

"You've been gone since eleven," she says.

"It was a long walk," you say.

"I followed you," she says. "You thought I was asleep. My eyes were closed, yes, but I was not asleep. When you left five hours ago, I followed you to an apartment building. Who is she?"

"Look," you say, but you know it's over and there's no way of talking yourself out of this.

"I can *smell* her on you," says your wife. "I've been smelling her for a while. I thought I was imagining it. I thought I was crazy. But this has been going on for a while now, hasn't it? I should've seen it. How long has this been going on?"

"A while."

"A month?"

"A year."

"A *year*?"

"Yeah."

"You bastard."

"I'm sorry."

"Who is she?"

You tell her.

"Oh," your wife says, "oh, I know her. Yes, of course. Why did you choose her?"

"I don't know."

"You have a week," says your wife, "the end of the week to have all your stuff out of this house. Then we'll talk lawyers."

"Be reasonable," you say.

"I am," she says. "I could kick you out right now."

NEXT: WRITE POETRY

You move in with the other woman and she's happy about this change. Now you can sleep in her bed. She's now a girlfriend, the significant other. Her divorce is finalized and she talks about a second marriage, when your divorce goes through. Her apartment is too small so you both rent a condo. Your divorce proceedings begin. It's hard to work on the genre novels so you work on a screenplay but your agent says, "Everyone writes those things and they're not as easy to sell as you might think; you might as well write poetry." So you start to write poetry.

Your girlfriend is not the other woman, the sex is no longer exhilarating and perilous. She seems bored with you as well. You flirt with her friends, hoping something might happen, and she doesn't appreciate this one bit. "Has it *always* been like this with you," she asks, "is there always a wife or girlfriend *and* another woman?"

"No," you say, and soon find yourself in a one-bedroom apartment. Your divorce is finalized and you're single.

THE RULES OF BEING SINGLE

You don't like being single, you have no idea *how* to be single. You hate sleeping alone, it's so damn lonely. You don't know how to meet woman and you've never been comfortable asking them out on dates. You suggest to your ex-wife something about trying it all over again, from scratch, but she says, "I'm seeing someone and I'm in love." You're still friends with an old ex-girlfriend from ten years ago and while she's willing to go out to dinner and such with you, to drink and talk and whatnot, she's not interested in a relationship. "You're not easy to be with," she says.

At a party, you meet a friend of this ex-girlfriend's that you feel is attracted to you. You're attracted to her. She's married but you know she's not happy, she's looking for something. You talk to her on the phone a few times but she says she can't see you, she's married. Two months later, she calls and says, "I'm separated now, I have my own apartment, I can go out on dates. I haven't gone out on a date in thirteen years."

After the first date is through, she shakes your hand, she doesn't invite you in, she says, "That was fun; let's do it again."

MAX ROD

On the second date with this woman, you go to a restaurant she says is her favorite. At the bar, waiting for a table, she runs into a married couple she knows. The couple look at you like you're a child molester.

"They don't know I'm separated," she tells you later. "So imagine their surprise when they see me with you. They thought I was having an affair!" she says with delight.

"Did you ever have an affair while you were married?"

"I had a one-night stand. It was at a conference—different city, a big hotel on the waterfront in the middle of summer. He was married, we were both very attracted to each other. I felt very guilty when I went home. I felt guilty for months. I told myself I'd never do that again, and I didn't."

She's very interested in your affair story—she finds it all very exciting. "I have such a dreadfully uneventful life," she goes. She wants all the details from you, especially about the sex—and you're good with the minutiae because you are presently writing porn novels under the name "Max Rod" for a book packager to pay the rent.

"So where are they now?" she asks.

You say, "My ex-wife is pregnant and is getting remarried; my ex-girlfriend is robbing the cradle—she's dating a nineteen-year-old college student."

"I would've never been good at it," the woman on the date says, "having an affair. Seems too complicated."

"It's easy when you're doing it."

ACKNOWLEDGMENTS

Some of these stories were originally published, in slightly different form, as follows:

"Karin" first appeared in *Fiction International*.

"Jolene" first appeared in *Red Hot Erotica*, edited by Alison Tyler.

"Natalie" first appeared in *Naughty Spanking Stories A-Z* edited by Rachel Kramer Brussell and *Luscious*, edited by Alison Tyler.

"Mo" first appeared in *C Is for Co-eds*, edited by Alison Tyler.

"Hollow Hills" first appeared in *The Mammoth Book of Erotica*, revised edition, edited by Maxim Jakubowski.

"Sandra Boise Turns Thirty" first appeared in *The Happy Birthday Erotica Book*, edited by Alison Tyler.

"Movements" first appeared in *Aqua Erotica*, edited by Mary Anne Mohanraj; as well as *The Mammoth Book of Best Erotica 2000,* edited by Maxim Jakubowski.

"Moments" first appeared in *E Is for Exotic*, edited by Alison Tyler.

"The Brilliance and Misery of Bodies; of War, of Dreams" first appeared in *The Mammoth Book of Historical Erotica*, edited by Maxim Jakubowski.

"Toys" first appeared in *A Is for Amour*, edited by Alison Tyler.

HOW TO HAVE AN AFFAIR, BY HEMMINGSON

"How to Have an Affair" first appeared in *Homewrecker: An Adultery Reader*, edited by Daphne Gottlieb.

I would like to thank the editors of these anthologies for publishing them first. I would also like to acknowledge the women I've known who inspired some the true stuff in these fictions: Karin, Christine, Beth, Rosina, Anya, Lisa, Liv, Dominique, Valerie, Sage, Lira, Katie, and Stephanie.

ABOUT THE AUTHOR

MICHAEL HEMMINGSON writes books in every possible genre he can: literary, western, SF, horror, noir, autobiography, erotica, narrative journalism, gonzo journalism, cultural anthropology, critical theory, critifiction, ethnography, and many other modes of academia including post-postmodern and post-colonial treatises. And private eye yarns. And film and TV studies. And smut. He also writes plays and screenplays. He has two independent feature films out: *The Watermelom* (LightSong Films) and *Stations* (Hemlene Entertainment). He has produced, directed, and written plays in San Diego and Los Angeles for the Fritz Theater and The Alien Stage Project. He lives in southern California, going back and forth from Hollywood to Ocean Beach, to Encinitas to Pasadena.